SUGAR CREEK GANG
7
The MYSTERY CAVE

Paul Hutchens

MOODY PRESS
CHICAGO

Original Title: *Mystery at Sugar Creek*

ISBN: 0-8024-7011-4

5 7 9 10 8 6 4

Printed in the United States of America

PREFACE

Hi—from a member of the Sugar Creek Gang!

It's just that I don't know which one I am. When I was good, I was Little Jim. When I did bad things—well, sometimes I was Bill Collins or even mischievous Poetry.

You see, I am the daughter of Paul Hutchens, and I spent many an hour listening to him read his manuscript as far as he had written it that particular day. I went along to the north woods of Minnesota, to Colorado, and to the various other places he would go to find something different for the Gang to do.

Now the years have passed—more than fifty, actually. My father is in heaven, but the Gang goes on. All thirty-six books are still in print and now are being updated for today's readers with input from my five children, who also span the decades from the '50s to the '70s.

The real Sugar Creek is in Indiana, and my father and his six brothers were the original Gang. But the idea of the books and their ministry were and are the Lord's. It is He who keeps the Gang going.

PAULINE HUTCHENS WILSON

1

The things that happened to the Sugar Creek Gang that dark night we all went hunting with Circus's dad's big, long-bodied, long-nosed, long-tongued, long-voiced dogs would make any boy want them to happen all over again, even if some of them were rather spooky and dangerous.

Let me tell you about our hunting trip right this minute—that is, as soon as I get to it. As you probably know, Circus is the name of the acrobat in our gang. His dad, Dan Browne, makes his living in the wintertime by hunting and trapping—catching animals whose fur is used to keep people warm and to trim hats and collars for women's coats.

Anyway, the Sugar Creek Gang were all invited by Circus's dad to go hunting with him that Friday night. We expected to have a lot of fun, walking by the light of kerosene lanterns through the dark woods along the creek, listening to the mournful bawling of the hounds on the trail of—well, most anything, such as raccoons, possums, and even skunks. We also all hoped we might run into another bear. Remember the one Little Jim killed in one of the other stories about the gang?

Friday night finally came, which is the best

night for a boy to be up late, because there isn't any school on Saturday and he can sleep late in the morning if he wants to. And if his parents want him to, which some parents sometimes don't.

Right after chores were done at our farm— we did them in the dark by lantern light as we always do in the late fall and winter—the Collins family, which is ours, ate a great supper of raw-fried potatoes and milk and cheese and cold apple pie and different things. Boy, it was good!

I looked across the table at my baby sister, Charlotte Ann, who was half sitting and half sliding down in her high chair. Her eyes were half shut, and her little round brown head was bobbing like the bobber on a boy's fishing line when he is getting a nibble, just before he gets a bite and *kerplunk* it goes all the way under and the fun begins. Just that minute Charlotte Ann's round brown head went down a long way, and my grayish-brown-haired mom, who has a very kind face and the same kind of heart, stood up, untied the cord that held Charlotte Ann in the chair, lifted her carefully, and took her into the bedroom to put her into her crib, which I knew had a Scottish terrier design on its side.

I felt proud to think that I knew nearly every kind of dog there was in the world, certainly all the different kinds there were in Sugar Creek, which is a very important part of the world. I even knew the dogs by name, but for some reason we had never had a dog in the Collins family.

Well, for a minute Dad and I were alone, and the way he looked at me made me wonder if I had done anything wrong, or if maybe I was going to and he was going to tell me *not* to.

"Well, Son," he said, looking at me with his blue eyes, which were buried under his big, blackish-red, bushy eyebrows. His teeth were shining under his reddish-brown mustache, though, and when his teeth are shining like that so I can see them, it is sort of like a dog wagging his tail. That meant he liked me, and there wasn't going to be any trouble. Yet trouble can happen mighty quick in a family if there is a boy in it who likes to do what he likes to do, which I did.

"What?" I said.

Dad's voice was deep, as it always is, like a bullfrog's voice along Sugar Creek at night, as he said, "I'm sorry, Bill, to have to announce that—" He stopped and looked long at me.

All of a sudden my heart felt as if some wicked magician had changed it into a lump of lead. What was he going to announce? What was he waiting for, and what had I done wrong, or what was I *about* to do that I shouldn't?

Just that minute, while Dad's sentence was still hanging like a heavy weight of some kind about to drop on my head, Mom came in from having tucked Charlotte Ann into bed. "I'll fix a nice lunch for you to take along in your school lunch pail, Bill. Apple pie, warm cocoa, sandwiches, and—"

My dad must have been thinking about what he was going to say and not hearing Mom at all. He went on with his sentence by saying, "Sorry to have to announce that Dr. Mellen called up this afternoon and said he would be ready for you to get your teeth filled tomorrow morning at eight. I tried to arrange some other time for you, but we had to take that or wait another week, so you'll have to be home and in bed a little after eleven.

"I've made arrangements for Dan Browne to leave you and Little Jim at Old Man Paddler's cabin, where Little Jim's daddy will pick you up. Little Jim's piano lesson is at nine in the morning anyway, so his mother—"

Well, that was that. Little Jim and I couldn't stay out in the woods as late as the rest of the gang. My heart was not only lead but hot lead, because I didn't like to go to a dentist and have my teeth filled, and I didn't want to come home till the rest of the gang did.

I felt sad and must have looked sadder.

"What's the matter?" Mom said. "Don't you like apple pie and cocoa and sandwiches?"

I was thinking about a cavity I had in one of my best teeth, and I was thinking about how I would look with a little piece of shining gold in one of my front teeth, so I said to Dad, "What kind of filling?"

And Mom said, "Roast beef and salad dressing."

And Dad said, "Gold, maybe, for one and porcelain for the others."

And Mom exclaimed, "*What* in the—" and stopped just as we heard the sound of steps on our front porch, and I saw the flashing of a lantern outside the window and heard different kinds of voices at different pitches. I knew the gang was coming.

In a minute I was out of my chair and into my red crossbarred mackinaw, with my red corduroy cap pulled on tight. I was making a dive for the door when Dad's deep voice stopped me by saying, "You forgot your manners again."

So I said, "I mean, excuse me, please. Where's my lunch, Mom?" Maybe I didn't have any manners at all for a minute.

My lunch wasn't ready, so I went outside and waited for it and for the rest of the gang to come. Our house was the place where they had all agreed to meet.

I say the *rest* of the gang because only two were there: Poetry, our barrel-shaped member, who knows 101 poems by heart, and Dragonfly, the spindly-legged member, whose eyes are too large for his head and whose nose is crooked at the bottom.

Dragonfly's teeth are also too large and *will* be until his face and head grow some more. And he is sometimes "seeing" things that are not there. The very minute I saw Dragonfly with his big dragonflylike eyes shining in the lantern light, I knew that something new and different was going to happen on our hunting trip—nothing to *worry* about, of course, but just to *wonder* about. I had enough to worry me by thinking of the dentist and the next morning at eight o'clock.

I had no sooner gotten outside than there was a whimpering sound at my knees. Looking down, I saw a tan long-muzzled dog with curly rough hair. It was sniffing at my boots to see if it liked me enough to wag its stumpy tail at me, which it did, only it didn't waste much time on me, because right that minute our black-and-white cat, Mixy, came arching her back along the side of the porch, looking for somebody's legs to rub up against. She and that tan dog saw and smelled each other at the same time.

The next thing I knew, a streak of brown and a streak of black-and-white were cutting a terribly fast hole through the dark on the way to our barn.

Dragonfly let out a yell. "Hey, Jeep! Leave that cat alone!" It was Dragonfly's new dog, which his parents had bought for him somewhere.

Just then Poetry's squawky, ducklike voice began quoting one of his poems. It sounded funny, and his round face looked funnier in the light of his lantern, which he was holding close, trying to see what was happening to the cat—or maybe to the dog, because old Mixy cat was a fierce fighter if a dog ever caught up with her. The poem went:

Hey! diddle, diddle,

The cat and the fiddle,
The cow jumped over the moon.
The little dog laughed
To see such sport,
And the dish ran away with the spoon.

"The dog ran away with the *cat*, you mean,"
I said.

Just then we heard a banging out in the barnyard, which sounded as if one of our cows had tried to jump over the moon and hadn't been able to make it on account of the barn or a hog house being in the way.

"You *certainly* aren't going to take that Airedale along with us on our hunting trip!" I said to Dragonfly.

"I *certainly* am!" he replied. Then he added, "And why not?"

It was Poetry who answered squawkily, "'Cause any dog that is nervous like that and goes shooting like a torpedo after a cat wouldn't be worth a picayune on a hunting trip. He'd have the hounds off the trail half the time, barking at rabbits in a brush pile or up the wrong tree or chasing somebody's house cat."

"What's a *picayune*?" Dragonfly wanted to know.

And because I'd had the word in spelling that week and had looked it up, I said, "A picayune is 'a person or a thing of trifling value.'"

Well, that little spindly-legged guy was peeved on account of what Poetry had said about his Airedale. He said saucily, "Here,

Picayune, give me that lantern a minute, and I'll go out and save the cat's life."

He snatched the lantern, which Poetry let him have, and started off to the barn *lickety-sizzle,* leaving Poetry and me alone in the dark, with the light from the house shining out across the porch on Poetry's green corduroy cap and his brown leather jacket.

The light also shone on his round face and his very big feet. Poetry had the longest feet in all the Sugar Creek Gang. He was wearing leather boots with rubbers on them to keep his feet dry because it was muddy in places and there would be plenty of wet grass and leaves and maybe puddles to walk and run in on our hunting trip.

The weather was just right for hunting, though, because when the ground is damp like that, the hounds can smell better, and the coons and possums and things leave their scent on the leaves and grass or wherever they walk or run or climb.

I had learned all that from my dad and from Circus himself. Besides, any boy on a farm knows these things.

Just that minute we heard galloping hoofs and a snorting horse. And then Circus came riding into our lane and up to our back door. The minute his pony slid to a quick stop, Circus kicked his feet out of the stirrups. In a split second he was standing on his hands on the saddle with his medium-sized feet balanced in the air, before he swung himself out over the pony's heaving side and landed on the board-walk beside Poetry and me.

"Hello, gang," he said. "Where's everybody?"

"I'm right here!" a new voice called from the path that ran through our orchard. Looking behind me, I saw a flashlight bobbing back and forth like the pendulum on our kitchen clock. It was two people, a tallish boy with his cap on sideways, and a short-legged little guy with his cap on backwards and with the bill turned up. It was Big Jim and Little Jim. Both were wearing rubber boots, and all of us were wearing mittens or gloves.

That was all of the original Sugar Creek Gang except for Dragonfly, who just that minute came galloping up from the barn, swinging Poetry's lantern. His Airedale dog was beside him and in front of him and behind him at almost the same time. The light of the lantern made so many shadows in different directions that Dragonfly looked like three boys with four dogs jumping around him.

There was one other member of our gang, Little Tom Till, who lived across the creek a half mile or so away and whose big brother, Bob, had caused us so much trouble. Tom Till had red hair and freckles like mine and wasn't ashamed of it. He and I didn't have any more fights, because I'd found out he was a better guy on the *inside* than showed on the *outside*, as lots of red-haired, freckled-faced people are—including maybe me, some of the time.

Just as I was wondering if red-haired Tom

was coming, Little Jim, who is my best friend in the whole gang except for maybe Poetry or Dragonfly, sidled over to me and, tugging at my arm, started to tell me something.

I leaned over and listened, and he said, "Tom Till's daddy is gone again, and nobody knows where. My daddy says we'd better—we'd better—"

"Anybody seen anything of Tom?" Big Jim wanted to know. Big Jim and Big Bob Till had been terrible enemies for a year or two, you know, but weren't anymore although they still didn't like each other very well and maybe never would. Big Jim was kindhearted though, and he was especially kind to Little Tom.

Big Jim's question stopped Little Jim from telling me the rest of what he was about to tell me.

"Tom can't come," Little Jim said.

Little Jim, I'd better explain, wasn't Big Jim's brother. They just happened to have the same first name.

Then Little Jim tugged at my arm again, and I leaned over again, and he started to finish his sentence again, and it was, "John Till is in trouble with the police, and Daddy says we'd better—we'd better—"

Just that second our back door swung open wide, and the light came splashing out across the porch and into all our faces. And my mom called, "Your lunch is ready, Bill! Oh, hello, everybody! They're all here, Dad!" she called back into our house.

My big strong dad came out onto the porch and looked us over with eyes that were almost buried under his bushy brows. He said, "Well, gang, have a good time. I'm sorry I can't go along, but I have some letters to write. When you get to Seneth Paddler's cabin up in the hills, tell him I'll be around to see him about Palm Tree Island tomorrow sometime."

"We'd better get going," Circus said. "Dad told me to tell you all to hurry up. That's why he sent me over—to tell you to step on the gas. The hounds are almost crazy to get started, and it may either rain or clear off or turn cold, and if it turns cold and freezes, they can't trail very well."

That was that, and Little Jim still hadn't told me what his dad wanted him to tell me— or us.

In a few minutes we were ready. Little Jim was riding on the pony behind Circus, and the rest of us were scrambling along behind. Dragonfly's crazy Airedale shuffled along all around and in between us. Dad's last words were ringing in my ears, "Don't forget, Bill, to tell Seneth Paddler I'll be over to see him tomorrow about Palm Tree Island."

That didn't interest us much except that we all knew that Old Man Paddler, who is one of the greatest old men that ever lived, had probably asked my father to send some money down there to some missionaries. Old Man Paddler was much interested in things like that.

Just then Dragonfly's Airedale darted in

between my legs on his awkward way across the road to give chase to a rabbit. I stumbled over him and over myself and went down into a small puddle.

"That crazy *dog!*" I exclaimed from somewhere in the center of the road. "What on earth do you want him to go along for?"

"That's what I say!" Poetry huffed from beside me. And—would you believe it?—he was getting up off the ground at the same time I was.

"He's a wonderful dog," Dragonfly said defensively. "Just you wait and see. He'll maybe catch a bear or a lion or maybe save somebody's life or something. I read a story once about—"

"Hurry *up,* you guys!" Circus called back to us from his pony, and we did, all of us starting to run to try to keep up with him.

Poetry, puffing along beside me, said between puffs, "I just know that curly-haired mongrel is going to get us into trouble."

"He's *not* a mongrel!" Dragonfly exclaimed behind us. "He's a purebred Airedale."

"He's a *picayune!*" I told Dragonfly. "He's a thing of trifling value."

"He's a *person!*" Dragonfly cried. "Here, Jeep! Here, Jeep!" he called. "Come back here and leave that rabbit alone! We're going *coon* hunting!"

Pretty soon we came in sight of Circus's sort of old-looking house, where there was a light in an upstairs window with somebody moving about, maybe turning down the covers for some of Circus's many sisters who lived there. He was the only boy.

Circus's dad and Big Jim's dad's hired hand, who lived close by, were there waiting for us with two more kerosene lanterns and a long, powerful flashlight and one long rifle. Tied close to the woodshed were two big, sad-faced, long-nosed, long-eared, long-bodied hounds, one a rusty red and the other a kind of blue-and-gray. They were leaping and trembling and acting like wild things, trying to get loose so they could go where they wanted to go.

Circus put his pony away in the barn, came back to where we were, and in less than three minutes we were on our way.

His dad, who had on a sheep-lined brown coat and high boots—as also did Big Jim's dad's hired man—went over to the dogs, scolded them so they would be quiet, and unsnapped their leashes. You should have seen them go, just like two streaks of greased lightning, out across the yard and over the fence and straight for Sugar Creek.

Maybe the dogs smelled something out there and knew just where to go, for we hadn't been following along behind them more than a half minute when one of the dogs—Old Bawler, the gray-and-blue one—let out a wild, long, sad bawl that sounded like a loon and a woman crying for help and running at the same time:

"*Whooo . . . whooo . . .*"

Then Old Sol, the red-and-rusty hound,

took up the cry, and his voice was deep and hollow as though it was coming through a hollow log in a cave and he was in a lot of trouble:

"*WHOOO . . . WHOOO . . .*"

"It's a coon!" Circus cried, and so did his dad and almost all of us, each one trying to be first to tell the other one what we thought it was.

"It's headed straight for Sugar Creek! Come on! Everybody!"

And away we went—lanterns, boots, boys, Dragonfly, Jeep, all running, *sloshety-crunchety, slippety-sizzle,* through the woods, over logs, up and down little hills, around brush piles and briar patches, panting and feeling fine and excited and wondering if it was a coon or a fox or what.

2

I couldn't help but notice that, just a minute or two after we had started, the dogs changed direction and were running not toward Sugar Creek but toward the little stream of water that we called the "branch" and which emptied itself into the creek quite a long way away from where we were.

It looked as if they were going to take us right back toward Circus's house, and we all followed along behind them, running or walking, whatever we had to do. Sometimes we had to hurry to keep up with the dogs, and then again we had to just amble along at a snail's pace because the dogs would lose the trail, going around a tree or a brush pile or something else.

"What do you know about *that*!" I heard Circus say. "That coon's going straight for our orchard!"

And it looked as if it was. It had left the woods. The dogs were far ahead of us. Jeep was darting in and out and around. First he would be with us, then he would be away up ahead with the "real" dogs.

The men were ahead of us, too, following the hounds, which had already turned and started toward Sugar Creek again.

Pretty soon, while we were walking along, I heard little Jeep barking all by himself. It was a funny sort of bark, entirely different from any he had barked yet. It sounded as if he felt he had done something wonderful. He wasn't ahead with the other dogs either. He was all by himself, barking up a little tree right at the edge of Circus's orchard. In fact, he was barking up a persimmon tree.

Circus, Big Jim, Poetry, Dragonfly, Little Jim, and I stopped to see what Jeep was after, which we supposed was a house cat.

Poetry squawked, "I'll bet it's one of Circus's sisters, and that picayune doesn't know the difference." Circus had many sisters, but he couldn't help it. For that reason he didn't know how to dry dishes very well.

I had Big Jim's flashlight, and I shoved its light toward the top of that tree and around it but couldn't see anything. Some of the leaves of the persimmon tree were still on. They were dark brown and not round and oval as they are in the summertime when they are large and shining and green. Now they were curled up the way old Jack Frost had left them.

Then my flashlight showed me, about halfway up, a strange looking little light-gray creature of some kind. Jeep was all around that tree now, barking and yelping and jumping up and down, scratching his claws on the thick, scaly brown bark.

Do you know what I saw when my flashlight was focused up there? Right in the crotch of a limb was *something* all right. The underpart of it was very dark. Beginning about the middle of its sides and going up toward its back, it was black-and-white, its fur mixed like a man's hair who is maybe about forty-seven years old. Its fur was nice and long.

The animal swung around a little then and shut its eyes against the light, and I could see that its head was a different color, a sort of yellow-white. Its cheeks were as white as the snow would be in another two weeks—or maybe even that very night if it should happen to snow, which I wished it would.

I knew right away what the animal was, because of its tail.

"Boy, oh, boy!" I heard Poetry say. "It's a possum!"

"Sure!" Little Jim said. "It's a big possum! Look at his little black ears, would you!"

"Those ears aren't black," Dragonfly said. "Not all black, anyway. See that little yellow streak up there on the tiptop of its ears!"

The fur on the underpart of this possum was dark, and it was also shorter than the rest, with just a few white hairs sprinkled in.

"I don't think it's a possum," Dragonfly went on to say, "because—look how black its legs are, and look how black its feet are."

I lowered my voice disgustedly. "It's a possum!"

I focused the flashlight on its tail, then moved the light right up the possum's body until the gray-furred little varmint scrambled around, turned his tail toward me, and began to climb on up the tree.

"See that tail!" I exclaimed. "That's what they call a prehensile tail!"

Big Jim, who was standing quietly looking on, said, "Here, Bill, let me have that flashlight!"

He had it almost before I could let loose of it, and he was directing the light still closer to the possum, reaching as high as he could.

Well, with all that noise going on, all of us jabbering to each other and Jeep barking and yelping, we forgot about Old Bawler with her loonlike voice and Old Sol with his hollow, gruff voice. We forgot all about Circus's dad and Big Jim's dad's hired man. We were excited because Jeep had proved that he wasn't such an ignorant dog, although I still claimed that he was a picayune.

So I said to Dragonfly, "It's just an accident that he ran onto this possum here."

"Yeah," Little Jim said, probably feeling like teasing somebody himself. "I bet he didn't know the difference when the possum's trail crossed the coon's trail, and he got off on this sidetrack."

"Sure," I said. "He thinks a possum is important."

Circus spoke up. "It *is* important! That possum is worth two dollars!"

Well, the possum was not interested in having us too close to him, so he squirmed on up the tree, reaching one long front leg after the other from one limb to another, and pretty soon he was going up very fast. I could see his long tail dragging along behind him.

"See his prehensile tail!" I exclaimed.

Dragonfly answered by saying, "What's a prehensile tail?"

As I told you, I'd been looking up useful words and learning how to use them by using them, so I said, "A prehensile tail is a tail that can hold onto things almost as well as a boy's hand can."

"A possum can hang by its tail as easy"—Poetry turned to Dragonfly, wanting to tell what he knew, too—"as easy as Circus can hang by his!"

Circus, as you know, was our acrobat.

Well, that was a bright remark, and we all had a good laugh.

"That," Circus answered gruffly, "is a bright remark without the glow!"

I heard a bit of scuffling behind me and looked around just in time to see Poetry beginning to get up off the ground.

Well, Circus decided it was time to go into action. He swung himself up into the branches of that persimmon tree and started up, hand over hand, after the possum. It was a funny sight to see Circus going up the tree following the possum and to see the possum hurrying and scurrying up ahead of him.

Still on the way up, he called back to us, "It's a good thing we are catching this possum. We've been missing too many chickens out of our chicken house!"

That was a fact. Possums eat a lot of different things that they shouldn't. They not only eat all kinds of insects in the summertime, but they are very destructive animals. Nearly every bird that nests on the ground around Sugar Creek has to be afraid an old possum will come along and tear up its nest and eat all the baby birds or destroy the eggs. Not only that, possums go right into people's chicken yards and chicken houses at night. If they get a chance, they will eat the little chickens too. And if it's a large possum, it will catch even the big chickens and eat them.

I remembered all that while Circus was on his way up the persimmon tree. He stopped once to pick and eat one of the little plum-sized yellow persimmons, which, since fall and frost had come, were ripe and tasted very good to boys and possums. But in the summer and early fall, they made your lips pucker if you tasted one.

Little Jim, who never liked to see anything get hurt, called up to Circus, "My dad says that possums are very good to catch all the mice on the farm, and they catch the moles too." That was just like Little Jim—always defending something or somebody, which maybe is a very good character trait to have.

Big Jim was holding his flashlight on the little gray varmint and on Circus, who knew that tree almost by heart and where every limb was. He'd climbed every tree on their place and almost every one along Sugar Creek, so he didn't have to wonder where the next limb was even if he couldn't see it. He just went right on up that tree.

"I'm going to shake him down!" he called back to us, and he started to do what he said he was going to do.

By that time, the possum was close to the top of the persimmon tree and was on the end of one of the branches, way out among the twigs.

Circus grabbed the small limb that the possum was on and started to shake it as hard as he could, holding onto the tree trunk with his other hand. I can tell you, the possum held on tight with his gray hair and his blackish stomach and his very black legs and feet. He even held on tight with his long, gray, round, tapering, prehensile tail.

But Circus knew how to shake possums out of a tree. He just jerked and shook and jerked and shook that branch and stopped and shook and jerked, and suddenly the front feet of that possum were loose. And then not only his front feet were loose, but every single foot was loose, and that clever gray-furred little rascal, who had his eyes shut because he didn't like to look into the flashlight, was hanging by his tail only. His back feet were reaching up, trying to clasp the limb his tail was still holding onto, the way a turtle's legs search all around trying to get hold of the hand of the boy who is holding it up by its tail—and also the way a crawfish's pincers do when you have hold of it somewhere.

Generally it does find your hand or finger just before you let go of it and it gets away.

Circus gave another quick, sharp jerk, but the possum just that second managed to get a grip on the limb again, and he scrambled up and onto it.

Big Jim threw up an idea to Circus. He called, "How about this? Maybe your dad wants that persimmon pruned up there a little!"

That was a good idea, so Circus had his knife out right away and decided that the possum's limb wouldn't be needed anymore. It was cut off in almost no time. Circus gave it a little shove, and out went Mr. Possum down through the outer branches of the tree to the ground. The minute he struck, he curled himself up into a ball the way they say porcupines do when they're about to be caught.

Well, Jeep didn't know what to make of it. He darted in there and started to grab hold of the possum with his teeth. Then he let go and jumped back. Then he dived in again and jumped back, and barked and panted and panted and barked and dived in again.

All the time the possum was still curled up in a ball, acting as though he was sound asleep.

"He's playing possum," Poetry cried, and that was true. Possums do that, you know, when they're about to be caught. They curl up into little balls, shut their eyes, open their mouths with a silly, sickly grin on their white faces, and look as if they are dead. Then if you leave them alone, they will run away.

Jeep darted in again, and this time grabbed the possum with his teeth, shook him as if he was a big rat, then jumped back, looking scared.

You couldn't wake up that possum, though. He lay on his side and had his head down between his forelegs. His sharp, long nose was almost touching his stomach, as if he was trying to protect his head or maybe to keep from getting bitten in the throat, the place a weasel likes to bite first when it catches a live supper.

Dragonfly spoke up then. "I wonder if he thinks he's safe just because he has his head down between his two front legs, like an ostrich does when it buries its head in the sand when there is danger."

Poetry answered him by saying with his ducklike voice, "Possums don't think. Possums *can't* think. Animals don't have brains enough to think."

"*Dogs* do," Dragonfly said, and it looked like the argument was in his favor.

We didn't have time to have an argument right then, though. Big Jim told them both to keep still.

Circus knew exactly what to do with a possum and how to kill it so it would die very quickly.

Little Jim turned his face away while Circus did that.

Then Circus took the possum by its prehensile tail and said, grunting a little, "He's pretty heavy to carry all the way. I think I'll lock him up in our woodshed. Come on, everybody!"

We all came on, following him up to their

weathered old house where we waited at the gate. All of us boys felt very bashful on account of Circus having so many sisters. Only one of them would even look at a boy with red hair and freckles. Her name was Lucille, and she wasn't afraid of spiders.

Pretty soon Circus was back again, and we all started to holler to each other, "Hurry up, or we'll never catch up with them."

Almost as soon as we were out in the woods again, we heard Old Bawler's high voice—and it sounded very far away—going "*Whooo . . .*"

A fraction of a second later, we heard Old Sol's baritone voice also bawling, "*WHOOO . . .*"

"I'll bet they've really found a coon's trail," one of us said to the rest of us, and we ran still faster.

"If it is a coon," Circus yelled to us, "we'll have a real fight on our hands."

3

It's a weird feeling—running *lickety-splashety-crunchety-sizzle* through the woods, panting and stopping for breath and hurrying on and climbing over rail fences and dodging around trees, not being able to see very far on account of the dark, and with everybody else around you or in front of you or behind you as excited as you are.

We could hear the bawling of the hounds and also the sharp, quick nervous barks of Dragonfly's Airedale, who was also in the coon chase, far ahead of all of us and running with the hounds.

When I caught up with Circus's dad and Big Jim's dad's hired man, I heard Mr. Browne say, "Any dog that will leave a coon's trail for a possum's can't be trusted."

And that's how we came to find out that the men had known all along that we were catching a possum back there.

"We thought we'd let the Sugar Creek Gang have some fun of their own," Circus's dad explained to us. "Besides, we couldn't leave the hounds on a trail like this one."

Just the same, the men wanted to know all about the possum, which we told them. We also handed each one of them a ripe persimmon, which some of us had filled our pockets with just before we'd left the tree. They were right about Jeep, though. He simply ran off on every sidetrack there was, diving in any direction after any rabbit that jumped up and ran.

But we couldn't let that spoil our fun. Boy, oh, boy! Bawler with her high-pitched voice and Old Sol with his deep gruff voice knew what they were doing, and they stuck to it. They kept their noses not more than a few inches from the ground, running this way and that, wherever the coon's feet had gone, and it didn't make any difference how many rabbits jumped in front of them. They acted as if a rabbit wasn't any more important to them than a crumb of bread that fell from a hungry boy's roast beef sandwich while he was eating.

Once, when for a while Old Bawler and Old Sol were having trouble finding the coon's trail, which they'd lost, Little Jim and I had a very interesting visit. And I found out what he'd tried to tell me about old hook-nosed John Till.

The hounds sounded worried as they tried to untangle the coon's knotty trail. They were jumping over logs and running around trees and splashing across the little stream of water we called the "branch" and splashing back again, whining and complaining and not bawling at all. They were acting like a boy when he is stuck with an arithmetic problem and his dad isn't there to ask helpful questions and maybe give an idea that will help him know how to work it.

It was while the hounds were having that

trouble that we all sat down and waited beside and on a big maple tree that had fallen in a summer storm.

One thing I had always liked to do was to go out into the woods along Sugar Creek—or somewhere where men were cutting wood—and climb up on the fallen trunk of a big tree and walk on it all the way from the base to the very top. Then, when I couldn't walk any farther because there wasn't any more trunk, I'd climb one of the upright branches at the top end, perch myself in a crotch of a limb, and sway back and forth and up and down, imagining myself to be riding on a cloud or in an airplane or maybe in a boat on an ocean or a lake.

So when Little Jim and I saw that maybe everybody was going to have to wait awhile till the hounds had solved their problem, we took Big Jim's flashlight and climbed up onto the maple tree trunk. Balancing ourselves, we started carefully to walk toward the top, maybe a hundred feet away, which pointed away from the little stream.

"'S'matter?" Little Jim asked me when we were by ourselves and holding onto each other and to an upright limb to keep from falling off the tree trunk.

"Nothing," I said. "Come on, let's go all the way."

"I mean," Little Jim said, holding onto me with both hands now and almost falling off at the same time, "I mean, why can't the dogs find the coon?"

"They've lost the trail," I said. "Old Mr. Raccoon knows we're after him, and he doesn't want to be a collar for any woman's coat, so he has maybe jumped out into the water and waded along awhile, and his smell has already been carried away in the current. Maybe he's a hundred yards down the branch and will climb out on the other side, or else he'll stay in the water till he gets clear to Sugar Creek, and then he'll find a safe place in a hollow tree and won't get caught."

By the time I'd finished explaining all that to Little Jim, we were all the way to the end. We perched on a branch, swinging back and forth and feeling fine, as good as if we'd just gotten our report cards in school and all our grades were As and Bs instead of what some of them sometimes are and shouldn't be.

"Do you know what I wish?" Little Jim asked me, and his voice was wistful, the way his mouselike voice is sometimes.

I expected him to say something very important, because Little Jim is the only one of the Sugar Creek Gang who has important ideas all by himself without somebody else thinking of them first.

Anyway, this is what he said: "I hope—" he stopped and gave his body a big lurch, and the tree limb we were on swayed back and forth, back and forth "—I hope we don't catch up with the coon. I hope it gets away!"

"What!" I said. "Why, Circus's dad could get maybe nine dollars for it, and that would buy flour and meat and fruit and—"

"Yeah," Little Jim said in a sort of trembly voice. "But just the same, I hope the coon gets away, and I hope Circus's family has flour and meat and fruit, too."

We rocked a while, back and forth, back and forth, up and down, and I was thinking that if Poetry were with us—and the branch was strong enough to hold him too—he'd probably begin to say in his half-boy, half-man voice,

> "Rock-a-bye, baby, in the treetop,
> When the wind blows,
>   The cradle will rock.
> When the bough breaks—"

That was as far as I got to think just then because Little Jim, whose father, as you maybe know, is the township trustee and knows all the important things that go on in the county, said to me, "John Till is running away from the police, and they are on his trail just like Old Bawler and Old Sol are on the coon's trail, and my dad says we'd better—"

Well, I knew that now I was going to hear what he had to say, and I had already guessed it would be something different from what most any other boy would say, because of Little Jim's being, as I told you, maybe the best Christian in the whole gang. So I wasn't surprised when he said, finally finishing the sentence he'd started an hour or two before, "We'd better pray [think of it—*pray!*] that the Lord won't let him get shot because he's not saved, and if he died he'd be lost forever!"

Right after Little Jim said that, everything was quiet for a while, neither one of us saying anything. I looked away a minute and thought of red-haired Tom Till, who had started to go to Sunday school right after I'd licked him in a fight and Little Jim had saved his life by shooting the fierce old mother bear that was about to eat him up. And I thought of Bob Till, who had had trouble with the police himself and was on parole now to Little Jim's dad. And I thought of their sad-faced mother, who had to sew and bake and wash for the family without enough money to buy things, all on account of hook-nosed John Till's spending nearly everything he made for beer and stronger drink.

I felt sad, and I thought a prayer to God that went something like this: *Please do something in the Till family that will help Little Tom's sad mom to be happy.*

Then I looked down the tree trunk through the branches, which still had some of their leaves on them, to where the men and the rest of the gang were sitting in the light of their lanterns. I could hear the splashing of the dogs in the stream, in and out, and I could hear them whimpering and their noses sniffling anxiously. I could hear a very quiet wind sighing in the trees above us, and I still felt sad inside. But at the same time I felt kind of—white—as if a little warm light were shining there, because maybe it does a boy good to pray for somebody besides himself.

Just that minute I heard a high, long-voiced bawl far up the branch. It was Old Bawler, who had found the trail again and was running in another direction. Then Old Sol's voice rolled out in a deep mournful sound, and the chase was on again. It wasn't until after Little Jim and I had unscrambled ourselves from where we were, all tangled up in the tree crotch and each other, and were following along with the rest of the hunters and Jeep, the picayune, that I realized that Little Jim had said something else and what it was.

"Do you know what I just prayed?" he'd said. "I prayed that if John Till had to get shot *first*, before he would repent of his sins, that God would let the police shoot him but not kill him."

Imagine that little guy praying a prayer like that!

While we were splashing along again on the chase, following the dogs, swinging our lanterns and flashlights, and I was wishing the time wasn't going so fast toward eleven o'clock and wishing I didn't have to go to the dentist tomorrow morning—while we were doing that, I began to feel weird in my heart, as if maybe Little Jim had prayed something very important. Maybe he was right. Maybe if John Till had a lot of trouble and maybe if he got scared terribly, he'd think about things and about how mean he was to his wife and boys and how selfish he was in spending all the money on himself. And maybe he'd—well, as Little Jim said, maybe he would repent, which means to be sorry enough for sin to actually confess it to God and be forgiven and saved.

Then I got to wishing that if something bad *had* to happen to John Till before he'd wake up —if he didn't have sense enough to repent without being made to—that whatever was going to happen to him would happen mighty quick for the sake of his sad-faced wife and his boys, who needed the right kind of dad as well as the right kind of mom.

I even wished that something would happen that very night while he was running away from the police who were on his trail like hounds on an animal's trail. John Till was so mean that he was almost worse than an animal —certainly worse than a possum or a coon, which doesn't know any better. *Old hook-nosed John Till did know better,* I thought.

Just that second I heard a shot from somewhere, and I knew it wasn't from any of us.

Dragonfly, who was in front of me, stopped dead still in his tracks, and I bumped squarely into him and into his dog, which was there also. "What was that?" Dragonfly asked.

Poetry, who had been puffing along behind me, bumped into me and said, "That? That was probably a car backfiring. That's a road over there. Somebody's car probably had to slow down for Sugar Creek bridge, and then when it started again, it backfired."

4

We didn't get to think any longer about hook-nosed John Till getting shot. Just that minute the dogs, including the little Airedale, started making more noise than ever, as if the trail was getting what is called "hot." That meant the dogs were getting closer and closer to the coon and might catch up with it any minute.

In fact that was what I heard Circus, just ahead of me, say. "Listen to that, would you? Hear Old Bawler bawl? The trail is getting hot!"

And so were all of us from running so fast, and even faster, down along the little stream toward its mouth, which is where it emptied itself into Sugar Creek and where Dragonfly and I once caught a very large black bass.

We were hurrying, hurrying, *splashety-sizzlety,* around logs and over logs and all around the little stream that we called the "branch," meaning it was a tributary stream, which any boy who studies geography knows about.

As I told you, I was trying to learn a lot of new words and how to use them by using them. I said over my shoulder to Poetry—who on nearly every chase had a hard time to keep up with the rest of us and was puffing along behind me

—"I hope the coon doesn't dive into the tributary again and lose his scent."

And Poetry, trying to be funny and not being, puffed into my ear, "Raccoons don't have any sense when dogs are after them."

Dragonfly, whose spindly legs were working terribly fast along on the other side of me, also tried to be funny and wasn't. He yelled, "They may not have many dollars and cents, but they can sense danger when they know dogs are after them"—which goes to show that even though we were excited, we were having fun.

Old Sol with his deep voice, which sounded as if it was coming through a long hollow log in a cave, was going "*WHOOO . . . WHOOO . . .*"

And Old Bawler, whose voice was high-pitched like a loon's or like a woman's screaming voice in a haunted house, was going "*Whooo . . . whooo . . .*"

"Hey!" somebody behind us called. "Wait for me!"

It was Little Jim, whose short legs couldn't work fast enough for him to keep up with us. All of us stopped except Big Jim and the men and waited till Little Jim whizzed up to us.

Poetry asked him, "Say, Little Jim, you know all about music. What key are those hounds barking in?" He held up his lantern so I could see Little Jim's half-happy and half-sad face and also see his cap that was still on backwards with its bill turned up.

Little Jim panted a minute and listened

before answering, then he said, "They're both in the same key, I think."

He really *was* a good musician, you know—his mom was the very best in Sugar Creek Township and played the piano in our church. Little Jim practiced hard every day, which is the way to learn anything anyway.

We all kept still while Little Jim acted as if he was thinking, which he was, and listening. Then he used his own voice and struck the pitch Old Sol's voice had been striking and *was* striking right that minute far down the branch. Then his voice jumped away up high to another pitch, like a bird springing up to a higher rung on a ladder, and he struck the same pitch as Old Bawler was striking every few seconds.

"*WHOOO* . . ." That was like Old Sol. "*Whooo* . . ." And that was like Old Bawler.

Then that short-legged little guy grinned and said, "Old Sol is on re in the key of F, and Old Bawler is on la in the same key!"

After that, I could see that Little Jim was more interested in the chase because he could think about the music in the dogs' voices. And if there was anything he liked better than anything else, it was music—unless maybe it was some of the sassafras tea that Old Man Paddler used to make for us when we went up to his cabin to see him.

We had started to go on when Dragonfly piped up from near us somewhere and asked, "What pitch is Jeep on?"

Well, Jeep was barking the way he always

had barked, every now and then, short and nervous.

Little Jim made us all keep quiet a minute, and then he said, after barking a little himself, imitating the picayune, "He's—he's off key!" There was a mischievous grin on his small face. "He's almost hitting *fa*, but he's sharp."

"See there!" Dragonfly exclaimed. "What did I tell you? I knew he was smart. Little Jim says he is." Dragonfly had never been very good in his music classes, not knowing that *sharp* doesn't always mean *smart*.

"I know what key your picayune is barking in," Poetry's squawky voice said in a very low key, and he winked at me.

"You do not!" Dragonfly said, angry at Poetry for calling his dog a picayune.

"I certainly do," Poetry said saucily.

"All right, Smarty, what key is he barking in?"

Poetry winked at me again and started to run toward where the dogs were all making more noise than ever. He tossed his supposed-to-be-funny sentence over his shoulder at Dragonfly: "Your Airedale is barking in the *don*-key!"

After that, the rest of us had a hard time keeping up with Dragonfly and Poetry. But Dragonfly was a pretty good sport, and even though he was mad, he could see that it was funny. So when he finally caught up with Poetry, instead of socking him he only said, knowing a *little* about music though not enough to get good grades in school, "Anyway, *you're* a shaped note and a round note at the same time."

And if you know anything about music yourself, you'll know that Dragonfly was a very smart little spindle-legged guy to think up a joke like that.

Things must have been happening up ahead of us where the dogs were and where the chase was hot and getting hotter, because all of a sudden, while my thoughts were all tangled up with music and notes and Little Jim and his mom and different music keys, the dogs' voices all at once sounded like a pipe organ in a church with a *kitten* walking back and forth, back and forth, across the black-and-white keys, the way our old Mixy, in fact, did across the keys of the organ in our own front room at home.

It was a very interesting half-dream I'd been having while being very wide awake, when things suddenly changed. That is, the dogs changed their tunes and their keys. All three of them were now barking like Picayune Jeep himself, all of them in short, sharp, nervous, and excited, *very much* excited, voices. Jeep sounded as if he was not only excited but as though he had done something wonderful and wanted us all to hurry up and come and see. In fact, they all sounded like that.

"Treed!" Circus cried beside me.

"Treed!" I heard Circus's dad yell up ahead of us.

"Treed!" we all called at almost the same time.

"What's *treed* mean?" Dragonfly wanted to know, but nobody answered him.

"What's *treed* mean?" he asked again, and Little Jim piped up across from him and said, "It means the coon has run up a tree to keep from getting caught on the ground, just like a possum does."

And that was right. Coons do that, just as Mixy does sometimes when a dog is after her. She goes like a bullet up a telephone pole or tree or our grape-arbor pole to get away.

We ran as fast as we could, every one of us, getting in and out of each other's way, until pretty soon I could see what we were all seeing at the same time. There was a round, tall maple tree, and around its base were the dogs, barking—not bawling, but barking in excited, staccato barks. I knew that *staccato* was the right musical word for it because just that minute Little Jim said, "Hear them! They're barking staccato now!"

And they were. Old Sol's deep, gruff voice sounded as if he had crawled all the way through his hollow log and was very happy about it. Old Bawler's high-pitched, quavering voice sounded as if she wasn't scared anymore. And Jeep sounded as if he knew he had been right all the time and had just found it out for sure and was bragging about it.

I tell you there was some excitement going on around there for a minute or two. The three dogs were jumping up and down, up and down, up and down, like hot popcorn in a hot skillet. Then they would stop barking for a little and just sit, tongues hanging out and panting, looking at us to see what we were going to do about things. Then when one of them would bark, another would, and also the other, and then all of them.

It looked as if there was certainly something up that tree all right.

Big Jim's dad's hired man snapped on his long flashlight and shot a beam of light up into the tree. He moved the bright, white round spot it made all around through the leafless branches, back and forth and around and around, making me think of a boy in our schoolhouse with an eraser, moving it across the blackboard to erase the chalk marks. Except that the light of the flashlight was erasing the *dark* off the blackboard of the sky. We could see every gray branch and twig of that tall old maple.

Suddenly I realized that beside me Circus's dad had his rifle ready, and I knew that in the next minute or two something was going to happen. I could feel it. The flashlight stopped moving and was shining on something dark. I knew it wasn't any squirrel's nest of dry leaves either. I knew that for sure when I saw it with my own eyes. Then Circus saw it, then Dragonfly saw it, being a little late for a change. Then all of the rest of us saw it just as plain as day— two little greenish-white-and-yellowish balls of fire away up in the top of the tree, and I knew we'd treed a coon.

We certainly *had* found a coon.

The very minute Circus's dad raised his long-barreled rifle toward the sky and pointed it directly toward those two marble-sized balls of fire—the coon's eyes—all three dogs stopped barking, stopped yelping, stopped even whimpering, and were tense, waiting for the sudden explosion that would mean the shell had been fired.

Well, I guess the dogs weren't any more excited than the Sugar Creek Gang was. We were waiting for the shot to be fired too. And all the time I was thinking about the coon, wondering what the *coon* was thinking about. Was it wondering how it would feel to be shot? I remembered what I'd said to Little Jim not very far back along the trail, which was that the coon probably didn't *want* to be a collar for any woman's coat.

Then there was the sound of Circus's dad cocking his rifle, followed by a few seconds of tense, careful aiming right toward the two green eyes. And then there was a loud explosion, which wasn't maybe so loud but seemed like it because everything else was so quiet. It was like a firecracker that a boy sets off on the Fourth of July.

And the two green eyes disappeared. The dogs, who had been sitting on their haunches looking up with every nerve tense, all of a sudden whimpered and trembled, waiting to see what would happen.

The next thing I knew there was a crashing

among the tree limbs. Then there was the sound of more crashing and still more. And down through the branches of that thousand-limbed giant maple tree came a brownish-gray object that for an instant looked half big enough to be a bear. And then it stopped falling. It must have caught hold of a branch and held on.

Big Jim's dad's hired man's flashlight was shining right square on it, and I got my first glimpse of a wild coon when it is scared and mad at the same time. Its large ears were as big as Mixy's. Its face was lighter than its furry gray-brown body, and I could see the white marking on its frightened face. Its nose was pointed, and its stomach was light colored. Above its eyes it was dark white, and below them it was light black. Just for a minute I had that glimpse of its face, for then it tried to scramble back up the tree, and that's when I got a good look at its tail.

Poetry, who is good in oral problems in arithmetic, said, "Oh, boy! *Look!* It's got—one, two, three, four, five, six, seven rings on its tail!" Of course, he couldn't have counted them *that* fast. Rings on a coon's tail are black fur rings that run all around its tail. The tail, except for the rings, is all a pale yellowish-gray-brown color, like the coon itself.

I wondered if it had been shot. Then I thought maybe it had been, because it seemed to lose its grip on the limb. It slipped and came down the tree trunk to the ground right in the middle of the excitement of barking dogs and jabbering boys and hollering men, who were scolding the dogs fiercely to keep them from leaping in and tearing the coon's beautiful fur to shreds so that it wouldn't be worth a cent to a furrier.

But you can't always get a dog—or a boy—to obey you right on the second, so those dogs, including Jeep, leaped into the fight. But old Mr. Coon—or Mrs. Coon, whichever it was—certainly was very much alive. It backed itself up against that tree and scratched out with both front feet the way Mixy does when she's mad. It hissed and spit and bit. It snapped at the dogs, and the next thing I knew I saw that the end of one of Old Bawler's dark, gray-blue ears was bleeding. Evidently the coon had caught her ear in its teeth, and Old Bawler, jerking away, had had her ear torn.

I tell you, the fight was on for good. There was a lot of noise—very, very *fast* noise—of men and boys shouting to each other and to the dogs and differently pitched and very excited dog voices barking at the coon and at the excitement.

But a fight like that never lasts long. Anyway, this one didn't because something happened that Circus's dad said hardly ever happens. That crazy coon—or wise coon, I don't know which—did something that only one out of a hundred coons ever do. It all of a sudden curled up into a ball, just like a possum—just as the possum we had caught had done—and pretended to be asleep or dead, maybe waiting for us all to leave it alone so it could run *lickety-sizzle* to get someplace and get away.

The dogs were surprised. They backed off and stood looking down at that silent bunch of gray-brown fur and panted. Their tongues hung out. Spittle ran out of their mouths, and their sides heaved fast.

Then Circus's dad and the hired man scolded them hard, and for a minute they obeyed.

"Aw, shucks," Poetry said. "It's another possum!"

"It is not!" Circus said. "It's just pretending to be dead."

And it was.

Circus's dad had his dogs trained pretty well, or they would have spoiled the coon's fur. But he used his fiercest, very gruff voice on them, and they slunk back behind him as if they'd been licked, the way dogs do when they feel sad. Circus's dad then caught them by their collars, and they behaved themselves, although they were still like racehorses waiting for a chance to dive in there and make short work of that coon. But it isn't any fun fighting somebody that won't fight.

Anyway, the rest of what happened right then isn't very interesting, only sad. Little Jim looked away, and I even did myself because I didn't want to see the coon killed.

Afterward, when we were all sitting in the shelter of a bluff with a nice friendly fire crackling and the flames leaping up toward the black sky, I sat beside Little Jim on a dry log we'd found under a ledge and watched the men skin the coon. I felt sad inside, but at the same time I remembered that Circus's family would have some money now to spend for food and clothes and things they needed.

Little Jim caught at my arm again, the way he always does when he wants to tell me something, so I leaned toward him, and this is what he said: "There's a verse in the Bible which tells about after Adam and Eve had sinned that the Lord Himself made coats of skins and clothed them."

I remembered reading about that in my Bible storybook, but I had forgotten it.

Dragonfly, who was sitting on a knot on the log on the other side of me, said, "What made Him do that? Didn't Adam and Eve have any other clothes?"

I'd never thought about that, so I said, "I guess not."

Poetry, who also had been listening and whose parents studied the Bible a lot, said, "If He dressed them in coats of skins, then some animal had to be killed."

I sat there thinking, watching the fire with its long, hurrying flames, and the sparks that were shooting up like yellow raindrops falling up instead of down. I kept watching the men skin the coon and wondered why animals had to be killed at all and why anybody had to have pain and such things as toothaches, and why there were such things as dentists in the world who wanted to fill people's teeth on Saturday morning at eight o'clock.

Thinking of the dentist and of my teeth reminded me of my lunch, which I'd managed to carry all that time without eating any of it and without dropping it, and I was very hungry.

Pretty soon the coon was skinned, and its beautiful fur pelt was folded into the big pocket of Dan Browne's hunting coat. And then Circus's dad said to all of us, "And now, boys, we are ready for the surprise—or *are* you ready?"

That word *surprise* was one I had always liked. I was ready for whatever was coming next. I was also hungry.

Then Mr. Browne picked up the carcass of the coon and walked over to the fire with it. "Anybody hungry?" he asked.

What? I thought. *He isn't going to cook—*

I was wrong, though, in what I had been thinking, and I saw something then that made me like Circus's dad a lot better. He stood there by the fire only a few seconds. Then he walked over to a little, bare, wild rosebush, which in the summertime would have had beautiful red roses on it, and I watched him.

He stood there with his back to us, and I could hear him sort of mumble, "Little old coon, I'm sorry, but you really *had* been eating too many of our chickens. Thank you, anyway, for your nice warm fur, which I've taken away from you. It will help me support my large family . . ."

I couldn't hear any more just then. But when I saw that great big strong man lay the coon's body beside the rosebush and turn around, I knew that he was a kind person.

There wasn't any smile on his face for a minute. Then he turned away quick and called out to all of us, "Everybody ready?"

We all were, and said so.

"Follow me," Dan Browne said, "and I'll show you."

I could hardly wait to see what the surprise was going to be.

5

I always had a hard time waiting for things to happen when I wanted them to happen right away. It wasn't very long, though, until all of us were walking along happily through the woods, following Sugar Creek, following the path that leads toward the old sycamore tree.

You'll remember that a lot of important things had happened around that sycamore tree. You'll remember that while the Sugar Creek Gang had been away on an airplane trip there had been a very bad electrical storm. We were up in the plane at the time, riding above the storm on our way to Chicago. When we came back from our trip and were playing around in the woods one sunny afternoon, Dragonfly, who is always seeing things first, had seen a big, ragged, jagged hole in the side of the hill right at the roots of the old sycamore tree.

Lightning had struck that tree and ripped its way right down the trunk, leaving a large, long, ugly, splintered white gash all the way to the roots and into the ground, where it opened up a cave. Well, you know the rest of that story —how we went into the cave entrance and found that it was shaped something like the inside of the mouth of a large catfish. You maybe remember also that one dark night we saw a ghost—or *something*—there.

There was a rock that was a hidden door, and when it was moved we had seen a black opening into the hill, which looked as if maybe it didn't have any end at all. That cave turned out to be a very long one.

We all went inside and—but that's another story, which I've already written, and I want to tell you now about what happened when all of us, including Jeep, the picayune, went inside.

Pretty soon we were beside the base of the sycamore tree, not far from the famous Sugar Creek swamp, looking at a big canvas curtain hanging in front of the cave's entrance.

"Looks like somebody's been here," Dragonfly said to me.

Somebody had, for there was an envelope pinned onto the curtain.

Everybody stopped, and Big Jim, being the leader of our gang, was delegated to see what the envelope had in it. He stood there with all our eyes fastened on him and unpinned the envelope, which had written on the outside "To the Sugar Creek Gang."

"Go ahead and read it!" Circus's dad said.

Big Jim opened the envelope and, with me holding a flashlight for him so he could see, he read. While he was reading, I noticed that the downy fuzz was on his upper lip again. I remembered he had just shaved it off less than two months before.

"Read it out loud," Dan Browne said.

And Big Jim did. His half-man's voice read:

"Members of the Sugar Creek Gang: Attention! A special sassafras tea party has been planned for you tonight at the Nest. Come in the back way!"

When I looked over Big Jim's elbow, I noticed that the note was written in Old Man Paddler's trembly handwriting, and he had signed his name, "Seneth Paddler."

"Whoopee!" Poetry cried. He was always hungry and always in for a good time. But we all felt the same way. We could hardly wait till we got inside that cave and were on our way along its narrow passageway up to Old Man Paddler's cabin.

We had our lanterns and flashlights, which would make it easy for us to see. In a jiffy we were inside the catfish-shaped mouth and looking through the hole where the big stone used to be. The inside of the cave was lined with rock as far back as we could see.

We started moving along Indian style, one at a time. The passage was too narrow most of the way for two of us to walk beside each other. Poetry, all by himself, had a hard time getting through one narrow place.

The dogs were following along behind. They had strange expressions on their faces as if they didn't know what in the world was happening and were going to follow us to see if it was safe. Jeep was acting sort of scared. Maybe he'd never been in a cave before in all his dog life.

I noticed that each dog wore a leather collar with a brass plate with "County Dog License" printed on it and also a number. Nobody in Sugar Creek County could keep a dog without a license. If any dog was found running loose without a license, it could be picked up by an officer and put into a dog jail, which is called a dog "pound." And unless somebody came and claimed it and paid for a license for it, that would be the end of that dog.

Well, we were walking along, walking along, walking along. Gravel and sand covered the solid rock floor. Now and then we had to stoop to get under a low place. Once we had to squeeze through a *very* narrow place between two rocks that jutted out.

All this time, though, in spite of the surprise, I kept remembering that I was supposed to *stay* at Old Man Paddler's cabin when we got there. I had to be there by eleven o'clock, whether the night of hunting was over or not. But it wasn't anywhere near eleven yet, so I joined in and had a good time.

Picayune Jeep stayed so close to Dragonfly, as though he was afraid, that it reminded Poetry of a poem by Robert Louis Stevenson. He quoted it:

"I have a little shadow
    that goes in and out with me,

And what can be the use of him
    is more than I can see.
He is very, very like me from my heels
    up to my head,
And I see him jump before me
    as I jump into my bed."

Then Poetry, in a mischievous mood, started all over again and said, so that Dragonfly could hear him,

"I have a little picayune
    that goes in and out with me,
And what can be the use of him
    is more than I can see.
He is very, very like me from my heels
    up to my head—"

And that was the end of the poem, on account of Dragonfly and Poetry's getting into a scuffle.

We kept walking along, everybody feeling fine, until pretty soon we came to a heavy wooden door.

Big Jim knocked while the rest of us waited. None of us were scared, because we'd been there before. I was thinking of that kind old man who liked kids so well and knew how to make them happy and how to make them better. He knew how to make a boy *want* to be a better boy.

I felt something tugging at my arm, and it was Little Jim again, wanting to tell me something. I leaned down and listened. And do you know what that short-legged guy with his little mouselike voice said? All this time he must have been thinking about the coon back there and the story in the Bible about Adam and Eve and how God had put coats of skins on them. Do you know what he said?

He said, "Bill, when we get upstairs into Old Man Paddler's cabin and are all sitting around his fireplace drinking sassafras tea and eating lunch, do you care if I ask him to tell us—" He stopped.

"Ask him to tell us what?" I said, looking down into his face, while Big Jim knocked again on the wooden door, trying to make somebody in the house hear us.

Little Jim finished his sentence. "Do you care if I ask Old Man Paddler why Adam and Eve had to have clothes made out of the skins of an animal?"

Just then we heard a sound as if somebody was coming down a stairway, and then a trembling, old, kind voice asked, "Who's there?"

Big Jim called through the door, "It's the Sugar Creek Gang!"

Wow! Those words sent a thrill through me. I liked the Sugar Creek Gang and was proud to be a member of such a great gang of boys, even if I wasn't so very much myself.

All the time I was waiting for the old man to answer and for him to open the door, I was trying to remember something, something I was supposed to do or say.

What is it? I asked myself.

I searched every corner of my mind, but I couldn't remember.

Then I heard a sound on the other side of the door, like a steel bar being slid out of its place. Next I heard the sliding of a bolt and the turning of a doorknob. The big oak door swung open, and there we were, all of us looking into the cellar of the old man's cabin.

It didn't take us long to get inside and up the wooden stairway and into his warm house, where there was a roaring fire in the fireplace and hot water on the little wood-burning stove, with the teakettle singing and steam streaming out its spout.

Big Jim put the trapdoor down again, and we all sat on chairs or on the floor, wherever we wanted to.

I guess I never realized how cold I was until I got inside that warm cabin and felt the heat on my face and hands. Dragonfly was sitting beside me on the other half of a cane-bottomed chair. The fire was crackling, making a very friendly noise. The fire and the singing teakettle were almost like music. I looked down at Little Jim, sitting close to Big Jim, who was leaning against a log beside the fireplace. It looked as if Little Jim was listening to the teakettle and the fire. He was also watching the hungry flames eat up the logs. Everybody was talking to everybody, with nobody listening to the rest of us, like the women of our church do sometimes when they come to our house to sew.

I didn't have much of a chance to get in any of the words I wanted to say, so I just looked around the room at the different things. On the stove beside the teakettle was a large steaming kettle holding some red woody roots of the sassafras shrub, which grew in special places along Sugar Creek. The hot water was already red, and I knew the tea was ready for us to drink—maybe had been for a long time.

I looked around at all of us. Remembering that Old Man Paddler had named his cabin "The Nest," a brand-new name that he'd just lately decided to give it, I got to thinking about all of us crowded into that one room, sitting or lying down in every direction. We were a strange-looking nestful of birds, all right. Poetry with his barrel-shaped body in its light-brown leather jacket still had on his green corduroy cap and high leather boots with rubbers on them. Right beside me—so close to me, in fact, that I had to hold onto the back of the chair with my right hand to keep from falling off—was Dragonfly with his spindly legs and his crooked nose, which I could see as plain as day in the mirror above the table right in front of me. He was grinning all around at things, and his two big incisors were shining, reminding me of eight o'clock tomorrow morning. There was also Little Jim, who had taken his cap off—he always remembered to do that when he was in a house, without being told to. There were mittens of different sizes and kinds lying all around everywhere—sixteen of them, in fact—and with Circus's dad and Big Jim's dad's hired man and Old Man Paddler himself, we certainly made a crowded nestful of hungry birds.

Some of the other things I saw as I looked around were very interesting. On the wall above Old Man Paddler's clean-looking bed at the farther end of the cabin near the narrow stairs that led up to the loft—where I had never been but wished I could go sometime—was an ancient flintlock with a very long barrel—the kind of rifle they used in the days when America had its Civil War. Hanging beside it was a cow's horn, called a powder horn, which was what they used it for—to carry gunpowder.

Hanging on another wall, just above a battery radio, was a large rectangular map of the whole world. It was spread out and tacked up with thumbtacks to the wooden wall. Old Man Paddler had pins with large heads of different colors stuck into the map in different places. There were yellow pins in China and Japan; red pins in some parts of South America; pins with black heads on parts of Africa; pins with brown heads in places such as Mexico and Brazil and in some of the islands just below Florida. On a little island named Haiti were black pins. On the long caterpillar-shaped map of Palm Tree Island were several light brown pins.

The minute I saw the name "Palm Tree Island" I remembered what I was supposed to remember to tell Old Man Paddler—I was supposed to say what my dad had told me to say, and that was, "Be sure to tell Old Man Paddler that I'll come up to see him tomorrow about Palm Tree Island."

I was waiting for a chance to say something, not telling him right away because everybody was still talking to everybody else and nobody was listening to the rest of us.

Maybe I ought to tell you that almost right away Old Man Paddler started pouring the tea for us. It had been steaming on the stove beside the teakettle, a nice red-colored tea that we all liked very much, especially Little Jim. On the table was a big bowl of sugar and cups and cups and cups, enough for the whole Sugar Creek Gang and the men and also for the dogs. I forgot to say that the dogs were lying on the floor, very sleepy, just dozing with their eyes half closed, half open. Maybe they were drowsy because they had been working so hard out in the cold. They were like some of the farmers who come to the Sugar Creek church in the wintertime. After being outdoors all week in the cold, they just go to sleep in church almost as soon as our minister starts preaching. It isn't his fault, because he always preaches a good sermon, which he has worked hard to prepare.

Anyway, the dogs were lying there almost asleep in front of the warm, friendly fireplace. A minute later the tea was all poured, the sugar was in, and every one of us was sitting there or half lying down or half sitting up. Some of us were at the table. The rest of us were just holding our cups and saucers on our laps or wherever we wanted to, because it was what is called an informal tea party.

There were cookies and cakes also. I was pretty sure Old Man Paddler hadn't baked those cookies. I remembered having seen some exactly like them in our cookie jar back home, and I didn't get to take any because Mom had seen me starting to and had said, "Bill Collins! Always ask me first whether you can have a cookie, because I might need them for company."

As good a boy as I was, I always had to worry about whether there would be enough cookies for company. I always hated to ask, even though I knew that if I didn't ask *too* often, I could nearly always have one—or even two.

It wasn't very much of a party, but Old Man Paddler's cabin was certainly a friendly place to be. That white-whiskered man with his twinkling gray-green eyes and his very thick-lensed glasses was the jolliest old man you ever saw. I used to wonder why he was so happy, because I'd seen some old men who were very crabby. I guess something I heard my dad say once was right, and that was "The devil doesn't have any happy old men."

I looked at Old Man Paddler, and I knew the devil certainly didn't have him and never would, because God had got him first. Old Man Paddler liked being a Christian so well that he'd rather die than not be Jesus' friend.

Little Jim was looking at me again. He

reached out with the toe of his boot and touched the heel of mine, and I knew that he was getting ready to ask the old man his important question.

I nodded my head to let him know I was ready and that it was the best time, because right that minute everybody was talking about the coon. In fact, Circus's dad was just taking the beautiful gray pelt with the seven black furry rings on its tail out of the pocket of his coat, which he'd hung up on a homemade wooden hanger near the door when he came in. He displayed it, showing Old Man Paddler what a beautiful thing it was, and we were looking at it and remembering the chase and the fight at the tree and the shot and everything.

Mr. Paddler was admiring it with his gray-green eyes. Suddenly he said, "That reminds me of a story about Old Tom the trapper." And before I knew it he had launched into a story, his bobbing whiskers and his trembling voice making Little Jim smile, because he was very fond of that friendly person. In fact, it looked as if Seneth Paddler had planned from the very first to tell that story and as if Circus's dad had asked him to tell it so that the Sugar Creek Gang could have a specially happy time on their hunting trip.

Anyway, it was a story that I won't have time to tell now, but it was about a trapper who was shot with an Indian arrow one morning when he was running his trapline. Old Tom had lived along Sugar Creek away back yonder in the days when Seneth Paddler and his twin brother were little boys. Sometime I'm going to have Old Man Paddler tell that story all over again to the Sugar Creek Gang, and I'll write it down in a book for you, maybe.

As soon as the thrilling story was finished, Little Jim's boot touched mine again. He was just ready to ask his question when Circus's dad looked at his heavy watch and then at the gray-blue hound and said, "Well, Bawler, let's go get 'em!"

Talk about a dog waking up in a hurry. I wish *I'd* get wide awake that quick when my dad calls me to get up in the morning—unless it's Saturday morning and there is a tooth to be filled. Old Bawler didn't even take time to stretch and yawn and make a weird little noise in her throat, the way most dogs do when they wake up. Bawler was up on four feet quicker than Circus can climb a sapling and was over at the front door of the cabin whimpering and scratching and looking back at Dan Browne. In very good dog language she seemed to be saying, "Well, what on earth are we waiting for? Why don't we go *now*?"

Then Dan Browne said, "Sol! Wake up!"

Old rusty-red Sol, whose voice out in the woods is deep and gruff and hollow, let out a kind of low whimper and slowly opened his red-brown eyes. He looked lazily up at Circus's dad, wagged his long tail in a slow, lazy wag, and shut his eyes again. I suddenly was remind-ed of a boy who had a rusty-red head of hair who sometimes did that same thing, and I decided I liked Old Sol better than I did Old Bawler.

The men and Circus and Big Jim got up noisily, took their coats and the lanterns and mittens or gloves, whichever they'd had, and we watched them go down the path from Old Man Paddler's door, the one that leads past his spring and his woodshed. It wasn't too cold to leave the door open a minute, so the four of us younger boys stood there watching the swinging lanterns and the shadows bouncing around in every direction. Jeep was begging to go too, trembling with excitement and sitting on his haunches beside the doorstep, looking up at Dragonfly for permission.

It didn't feel very good to know we couldn't go along, but then I reckon one boy can't have *all* the fun there is in all the world, and he ought to be glad he gets as much as he does. But I tell you, a red-haired, ruddy-complexioned, seventy-five-pound boy can certainly take a lot and still be hungry for more.

I felt a strange lump in my throat, knowing that I couldn't go. For a half minute I was mad at my dad for letting the dentist make that date for me at eight o'clock in the morning. I was also angry at the dentist.

Just before we shut the door and went back into the cabin to wait for Little Jim's dad, I heard from away out in the woods and far up the hill a long, high-pitched dog howl that sounded like a loon and a trembly-voiced hoot owl at the same time, and it was Old Bawler striking a new trail. "*Whooo!*"

Then as if she had called across the valley to Old Sol, we heard him answer in his long, sad, gruff baritone, "*WHOOO!*" and we knew another chase was on.

We listened a while, then went inside, shut the door, and began what we supposed would be a very sad half hour of waiting for Little Jim's dad to come and get him and the rest of us.

Anyway, I thought, when we were inside and sitting or lying down on the friendly floor beside the fire in the fireplace, *Little Jim can ask about Adam and Eve.* I was getting curious to know the answer myself, mainly, I suppose, because Little Jim was so anxious to know.

Maybe we could turn on the radio, I thought, and listen to a program. I suggested it to Old Man Paddler.

He went over to the radio and was just going to turn it on when we heard steps, and I knew they were coming from the cave entrance to the cabin. Only they were running steps instead of walking steps, as I knew Little Jim's dad's would be, and there wasn't any knock at the wooden door down there in the cellar. Instead, there was something else.

There came a banging and a banging and a man's excited voice calling, "Let me in! Open up and let me in! Quick!"

6

O pen up and let me in! Quick!"
      Those rough, scared words sounded like
—who *did* they sound like they belonged to?

I looked at Little Jim's mouselike face, and
he was sitting with his fists doubled up. He
looked around quick and reached for his stick,
which he nearly always carries. It was lying
beside him, a striped stick with half the bark on
it and half off, making it look like a long piece
of dirty stick candy. He grabbed up that stick,
and right away he looked and probably felt
braver.

Dragonfly's dragonfly-like eyes were wide
open. *His* fists were doubled up.

Poetry just looked puzzled, as if he had
been shocked. I wondered if he was trying to
think of a poem and couldn't.

Jeep, the picayune, was standing straight
up on his four legs, with his stub of a tail also
straight up. He looked as though he was going
to be very brave. His voice had a deep, gruff
growl in it, and he barked a low, savage bark,
which was half bark and half growl. The rough
brown-tan hair on his back was doing most of
his talking for him, and it said, "I'm mad! I
won't let anybody tear anybody's door down
without putting up a fight!"

Again there came that scared pounding on the cave door down in the cellar.

Old Man Paddler, who had been stirring up the fire, turned around quick and said, "Sh! You boys go upstairs. Sh! *Quietly*! I'll handle this. Hurry, but no noise!"

I certainly didn't want to go upstairs, not when there was going to be the sort of excitement I knew there was going to be. The kind voice of Old Man Paddler had disappeared, and it sounded as if he meant business—like my dad's deep voice sounded sometimes when his bushy eyebrows were down.

As much as I hated to do it, I followed Little Jim and Dragonfly upstairs to the loft. And Poetry followed me, none of us being able to do it very quietly.

It was dark up there, but we could see a little by the light coming up the stairs from the kerosene lamp on the mantel and also because there was a crack or two in the floor up there.

I could see a cot and a dresser and some boxes and a writing desk and an old spinning wheel and different things like that.

I'd forgotten about the Airedale, but we needn't have worried about him. When he saw us all scrambling up that rough stairway, he must have decided it was a good place to be, because there he was, right next to Dragonfly. Except that he wasn't keeping quiet.

I thought maybe I ought to take charge of things up there, so I imagined how Big Jim would have done it, and I said in a harsh whisper, "Everybody keep quiet and don't move or whisper or anything!" It felt good to give orders like that, and for a second I was a general in an army and everybody was obeying me. Me! I felt important and as if I was more than I am.

I peeped through the crack in the floor that was right under my eyes. I could see the whole room—the many cups and saucers, not yet washed; the fire crackling in the fireplace; the teakettle on the stove, with steam coming out lazily because it was on the back of the stove; the radio and the map of the world; and Old Man Paddler, with one hand on the iron ring in the floor, pulling the trapdoor up. Then I saw the dark hole that was the cellar, and the wooden steps going down.

"Just a minute!" his voice called down the cellar stairs, and it was a very businesslike voice, not a bit scared. This was a different Old Man Paddler than I had seen before, and I thought more of him than ever. Just the same, I didn't want him to be alone with somebody who might be a criminal, or he might get hurt.

I stayed close to the stairway and took hold of the other end of Little Jim's stick, just in case the old man might need help. It wouldn't take me more than seconds to get down those steps.

I was trembling as badly as Jeep was. I could feel the other end of the stick trembling a little too, and I knew what that meant.

Just then Dragonfly whispered, "Listen!"

I listened, and Dragonfly whispered, "That's old hook-nosed John Till's voice!"

First, I heard Seneth Paddler's question as he called from down in the cellar, "Who's there?" Then I heard the scared answer, "It's John Till. Let me in quick. I'm c-cold. I'm nearly frozen."

It was a cold night, but not that cold, I knew. But then, he might not have on many clothes.

Anyway, I wasn't as scared as I was before, although John Till and I weren't very good friends. We hadn't been since I'd had a fight with him once in our oats field when he had given Circus's dad some whiskey. I had been so angry that day that I'd jumped in to help Circus and had plastered first one and then the other fist all over his crooked nose for almost four seconds before he whammed me on the jaw and ended the short fight. I never did forget that.

I lay there, glued fast to the upstairs floor, my eyes watching that trapdoor, my ears grabbing every sound they could. I heard the opening of the wooden cave door, the squeaking of the hinges, and John Till's voice saying, "Thank you." I was surprised to hear him say that.

A little later, John came up the stairs first, a big, ugly-looking man with a crooked nose and mussed-up hair that stuck out from under his black felt hat, which was pulled down tight onto his forehead. He had a flashlight in his hand. It was still on. He was wearing boots that were muddy and looked as if he had been in the swamp down by the sycamore tree. He didn't have on any coat, so I knew he really was cold. He slumped down into a chair just as soon as Old Man Paddler came up and closed the trap-door, and he stretched his gloveless hands out toward the fire.

The next thing I saw was Old Man Paddler pouring a cup of sassafras tea—first getting a clean cup from the cupboard—and giving the tea with a sandwich to that hungry, trembling man.

John Till wasn't saying a word, but he kept looking around as though afraid of something. I was glad the teakettle was singing a little, because we upstairs certainly weren't too quiet. I could hear us breathing and feel my heart beating and the other end of the stick shaking. And I could smell the Airedale, who was too close to my nose, and also the sassafras tea from downstairs.

And then I saw John Till jump as if he had heard something.

"That was just a dead branch falling from the old pine tree out there," Seneth Paddler explained. "Have another cup of tea? Here, here's another sandwich left over from—you're probably hungry."

You should have seen that man eat. He almost grabbed the sandwich off the plate.

My own lunch was still down there beside the fireplace. I hadn't eaten it on account of there had been enough other food prepared for us.

Pretty soon Old Man Paddler, who was sitting beside his table, reached up to the mantelpiece and took down a black book and laid it on the table, close by one of his elbows. I knew what kind of book it was, and so did Little Jim, who must have seen too because he pressed my arm.

Mr. Paddler's voice was kind again now, since he knew who it was and saw that John Till wasn't going to hurt him.

"Mr. Till," he said, "your son Bob is turning out to be a very respectable boy. We're proud of him, and I know you must be too."

And do you know what? I heard a kind of half sob in old hook-nosed John Till's throat as he answered huskily, "Something's changed him, and I guess maybe it's you. You—"

"No, not I," the old man said, and Seneth Paddler reached out a hand and put it on John Till's shoulder. "It's the power of the—"

I knew exactly what he was going to say, and so did Little Jim and maybe Poetry, because they both put their hands on my arm at the same time. I knew the old man was going to say it was an almighty power that had changed Bob Till, because that was the way he believed and the way it was.

"It's the power of the Lord, John—the same power that will come into your life too, if you will give Him a chance. There isn't anything too hard for Him."

Old Man Paddler hadn't any sooner said that than John Till's old black hat came off and he bowed his head. I actually saw several great big tears tumble out and splash down on the rough wooden floor right beside the ring in the trapdoor.

I couldn't believe my eyes. It couldn't be! *Not old hook-nosed John Till,* I thought. People like him didn't ever change. They just kept on being wicked and mean, and then they died and—

And all the time, Seneth Paddler's gnarled old hand was on his shoulder. "Listen, John" — I could hear tears in Mr. Paddler's voice, and I knew he not only liked that mean man but even more than that— "listen, John, I wonder if you would be willing to let me pray for you right now. Your two boys ought to have a Christian father, and Mrs. Till has a right to happiness, which she'll never have unless—"

John Till shook as if he was still cold.

That's what Dragonfly thought was wrong when he whispered into my right ear, "He's got a chill and will maybe get pneumonia."

It wasn't a chill, though.

"Look here," Old Man Paddler said kindly, and there in front of my eyes and right straight in front of John Till's eyes was the old man's open Bible. He began reading in a voice that still sounded as if it had tears in it. And this is what we who were upstairs heard—a part of it anyway, because we couldn't hear very well. It was "Whoever will call upon the name of the Lord will be saved."

For a minute I thought I was going to see

John Till bend his rusty knees and actually get right down beside that fireplace and do what the verse in the Bible said for him to do.

But then he straightened up, shook his head, pulled out of his hip pocket a red bandana, wiped his eyes, blew his nose, and said, "Not tonight. No, I can't do it! I ain't goin' to be a coward while the police are after me. I ain't goin' to be weak and turn to religion now."

Right that minute, when Old Man Paddler was about to show him another verse, I heard a sound outside. It was a little like a limb falling from a pine tree and a little like something else.

I wondered if it was eleven o'clock and Little Jim's dad had come for us.

John Till must have heard the sound too. He jumped, looked up, and his face had a hunted look. He leaped to his feet and looked all around as if trying to see a place to hide. Then he saw the stairs to the loft and said huskily, "You've been kind to my boy. Now be good to me. Let me hide here tonight. And if they come, you tell 'em I'm not here. Tell them you haven't seen me at all. Tell 'em—"

There was another sound outside, like men's voices, out by the spring and coming toward the woodshed and the house.

John Till shuffled toward the wooden stairs and took two or three steps up.

I don't know why on earth I had to sneeze just then or why Jeep had to growl a low, deep, savage growl, but those two things happened.

"*Achoo!*" I went.

"*Grrr . . .*" went the picayune.

John Till stood stock still and looked all around the room. The next thing we knew he had made a dive for the trapdoor to the cellar, had pulled it up, and a second later was down the stairs.

The heavy oak door down there opened and shut with a bang, and I heard running footsteps going back into the cave toward the old sycamore tree.

7

Squeak! Bang! *Crunch, crunch, crunch, crunch.*
That was the way the exit of old hook-nosed
John Till sounded to us.

It didn't take us long to get downstairs.
When I reached the bottom of the steps, Poetry, Little Jim, and Dragonfly were all there. In
fact, Jeep was down there too before I was.

Old Man Paddler was standing beside the
table looking surprised. In his left hand was his
black Bible. I think I never saw a man with such
a disappointed expression on his face.

"Well, boys—" he began, then stopped. We
looked into his eyes, and all the twinkle was
gone out of them. There was a tremble on his
lips, which I couldn't see but which I knew was
there by the way his long white whiskers were
trembling.

I don't know why I'd thought I had heard a
sound of voices. We opened the door and
looked out and called, but there wasn't any
answer.

I decided it was my imagination making me
think the police were there. I was just remembering what Little Jim's dad had told him, I
thought—that the police were after John Till—
and Little Jim had told me that we ought to
pray for him. And I had the thing all tangled

up in my mind, so that when I heard the sound of falling limbs from the old pine tree outside, I supposed that it was voices. On the other hand, maybe there *had* been voices. I didn't know.

But while we were standing there with Seneth Paddler, shuffling our nervous feet and looking down the cellar steps, knowing that John Till had run away, I got to wondering if he might bump into Little Jim's dad, who was supposed to come for us any minute. Or maybe the police *were* on his trail and would be waiting for him there at the door to the cave, and John Till would get caught after all.

I really felt sorry for him.

"Well, boys, I guess we've made a mistake," Old Man Paddler's trembling voice said to us. "We'll have to pray for Bob Till's father." When he said "Bob's father," I knew that one important reason he wanted John saved was for his boys' sake.

We put the trapdoor down again and sat in chairs around the fireplace. I opened my lunch pail and divided up everything for everybody, and we waited for Little Jim's dad to come, not knowing which door he would use. All of a sudden while the five of us were sitting there, Little Jim piped up with the question he'd been wanting to ask for a long time.

"Say, Mr. Paddler, while we were watching the men skin the coon, we got to wondering about the story in the—in the Bible where God made some coats out of the skins of animals and put 'em on Adam and Eve. We wondered why He did that."

Well, Old Man Paddler listened to that little fellow ask that question, and I could see right away that he wanted to tell us the correct answer. Nothing made him more happy than for a boy to be interested in things like that. So he smiled—I could tell he was smiling, because the twinkles were in his eyes again—as he sat there on his chair beside the table. He opened his Bible and turned to the first part of it, the book of Genesis, at the right place.

He began to read to us the whole story and to explain as he went along that Adam and Eve were the very first people there were in the world and that all of us are descended from them.

Dragonfly said, "I thought the cavemen were the first people there were in the world."

The old man looked at him over the top of his glasses and said, "Boys, remember one thing as long as you live. The first man in the world was Adam. As far as cavemen are concerned, there are people in some parts of the world who live in caves *today*. I know, because on my trip around the world I saw some of them. And there are people in some parts of the world who still live in *trees*, right in this very world in which all of us live." I knew that was even in one of my schoolbooks.

Then the kind old voice went on explaining to us. "Maybe I'll never have a chance to tell you boys this again, but I want you to remember it as long as you live. You all know the story of the cross and of the One who was the Son of God, who hung there one day out on a hill called Calvary. You know how His blood flowed out of His veins. The Bible says, 'The blood of Jesus His Son cleanses us from all sin.'"

While Old Man Paddler was telling us that story, I listened carefully, and it seemed for a minute that I was standing way back there outside Jerusalem at the foot of the hill in front of the cross, looking up toward the blue sky. I could see the face of the Man he was talking about, bloody under the hot, thirsty sun. I could see the two thieves, one on either side of Jesus. I could see the heat waves trembling above the top of the crosses the way they do on a sweltering day over the cornfields along Sugar Creek. I could see the people standing there in their different colored clothes.

In my mind I could see the blood flowing from the wounds in Jesus' hands and feet where the spikes had been driven through into the wooden cross. And all of a sudden I began to love Him very much, because I knew the Bible says that while He was hanging there He was dying for the sins of the whole world. And that meant He had done it for me and for all the rest of the Sugar Creek Gang. He had also done it for John Till.

Well, the old man's story went on. Everything was very quiet there in the cabin. All we could hear inside, besides his friendly voice, was the crackling of the fire in the fireplace and the sizzle-sizzle of the teakettle. We could hear the wind sighing in the pine trees outside.

My thoughts rambled around a little, getting all mixed up with the sound of the fire and the wind in the trees and the teakettle. It seemed I could still hear the *crunch, crunch, crunch* of John Till's shoes as they hurried away down the cave. Then for a minute it seemed I could hear the footsteps of one of Jesus' disciples, a man whose name was Judas. When he realized how he had betrayed Jesus, he ran away to hang himself. I could sort of hear *his* footsteps also, going *crunch, crunch, crunch* as he hurried out of the city. *Crunch, crunch, crunch* . . . until their sound disappeared.

Then the story the old man was telling made my mind swing back across thousands of years to the first two people there were in the world, and I was standing in a beautiful park-like garden.

I didn't expect Little Jim to interrupt him right then. He did it so quickly that I was surprised when he asked, "Did He make the coats of skins for Adam and Eve so they'd have a cover for their—for their *sins,* maybe?"

The old man, who had been talking with his glasses on so he could read when he wanted to, looked up at all of us and took off his glasses so he could see *us* better. Then, maybe guessing which one of us had asked the question, he said, "That's right, Little Jim, until someday His only Son came to take them away."

It was the easiest thing in the world to listen to that story, though it was a little too long for me to tell all of it here for you. But somehow I was glad a man like John Till (or even Bill Collins) had Someone on his trail, tracking him everywhere he went—not to hurt him or kill him but to *save* him.

And I was glad all those people back then had had an object lesson so it would be easy for 'them to understand that someday there would be a real Savior.

Well, it was a great story—though, as I said, a little too long and hard for me to remember all that the friendly, white-whiskered old man said. But we listened to it, and we understood. And I wished John Till had heard it. I wished all the people in the world could hear and understand it.

Suddenly Little Jim said, "What are all those colored pins over there on the map for?"

Old Man Paddler stood up, then sat down, and began to talk about the map of the world. "Well, boys," he began, "it's a little secret which I haven't told anybody about. I wanted all the Sugar Creek Gang to be here at the same time to hear about it, but I can tell you tonight, anyway."

Do you know what the pins on that map were for? He had a pin on it for every missionary he was praying for—a yellow pin for missionaries in China, the black-headed ones for those who were missionaries to Africans, the brown for those who were missionaries to people who were brown-skinned, such as many who lived in Mexico and South America and Palm Tree Island.

And all of a sudden I remembered what I was supposed to tell Old Man Paddler, so I said, "My dad said for me to remember to tell you that he was coming up to see you tomorrow to talk to you about Palm Tree Island."

The old man sighed, smiled, stood up, and walked over to the map like a teacher in a schoolroom. He pointed with one of his long, bony fingers at caterpillar-shaped Palm Tree Island, and he said, "Boys, I want you to keep your eyes on that place, look it up in your geography and history books and encyclopedias, and be ready for action. I'll have a surprise for you one of these days."

That's all he said, but there was a mysterious something in his voice that made me feel good.

"What kind of surprise?" Little Jim wanted to know.

"What kind of surprise?" barrel-shaped Poetry beside me asked courteously. Poetry had a very serious look on his face because at home he had a scrapbook in which he kept pictures of missionaries and maps and things telling about them. His parents were especially glad he wasn't making a scrapbook of movie stars and things like that. For all his mischievousness, Poetry had a good mind that could think serious things, even though you couldn't always tell it.

"Well . . ." Again there was a mysterious something in the trembling old voice. He said, "Boys, how would you like to go down there one of these days?"

I felt my heart leap and start off on a fast race as if it was going somewhere all by itself. I remembered that the old man had sent us on a camping trip up north, paying all of our expenses just because he liked boys so well and because he wanted us to learn a lot of things about first aid and about camp life and about the New Testament, which his nephew Barry Boyland taught us on that trip. I knew that Old Man Paddler had spent some of his money to send the whole Sugar Creek Gang to Chicago, where we'd had a wonderful time. And I knew also that he had a lot of money that he wasn't wasting on himself but that he was willing to spend on different people.

So do you know what I got to thinking? I got to thinking that maybe that generous-hearted old man was planning for the Sugar Creek Gang to someday go down the east coast of Florida and maybe get on a boat or a plane and go away over almost one hundred miles of ocean to that beautiful little place called Palm Tree Island. Poetry once told me Columbus thought it was the most beautiful island in the world.

I wished it, and I wished it, and I wished it.

Pretty soon it was eleven o'clock and time for Little Jim's dad to come for us. Then I heard a sound of steps on the twigs outside and a knock on the front door, and it was the one I thought it was.

Little Jim's dad, as you know, was the township trustee and had to look after boys who played truant from school and such things as that. He was a fine person, whom all of us liked very much. He was the one who was especially kind to Big Bob Till, John's oldest boy, and he was the one to whom the government had paroled Bob. He came in, and we all got ready to go home.

Old Man Paddler let us go through his cellar to take the shortcut to the sycamore tree, which saved a lot of walking, although eight o'clock in the morning would come just as quick, no matter how long it took us to get home.

We opened the solid oak door in the cellar. With our flashlights and with Jeep, the picayune, we started to walk through to the tree at the mouth of the cave. It looked as if our fun for the whole evening was over, so we started telling Little Jim's dad about John Till and all the different things that had happened.

"We caught a possum all by ourselves," Dragonfly said. "Jeep treed him, and Circus climbed the tree and—"

"Jeep got onto a sidetrack," Poetry said, going on with the story from where he had made Dragonfly leave off. "And there happened to be a possum close by, which looked like it wouldn't hurt a picayune, so he ran away from the coon and chased the helpless possum up a persimmon tree."

That was the way everybody felt—happy and cheerful. All except Bill Collins, who wondered how *many* teeth would have to be filled and who wished he had drunk more milk the past year or two and not had so much candy, so that his teeth would have been better.

We came to the canvas at the mouth of the cave, pushed it aside, and stepped out into the world again. And there we were by the side of the lightning-gashed sycamore tree. We hadn't any sooner gotten outside than Jeep, the picayune, pricked up his weird-looking ears and acted as if he was hearing something. Then he sniffed the air and acted as if he was smelling something. Then he swung his head around and looked straight ahead of where his nose was pointing, away out into the dark, as if he was seeing something. The rough brown and light-brown curly hair on his back started to move and stand up a little.

He began to growl first, then to bark in his throat. Then like a shot he swished out through the woods as fast as he could go toward the path that leads through the swamp. Away out there somewhere he started to bark fiercely as if he had something treed or there was a rabbit in a brush pile.

Dragonfly, standing next to me, raised his excited voice and yelled, "Come back here, Jeep. You crazy picayune! Leave that rabbit alone!"

But that little Airedale had a strange sound in his nervous voice. He didn't seem to be barking at a rabbit but maybe at something he'd never seen before, something very important!

"Jeep!" Dragonfly cried again, but his voice was swallowed up by Jeep's yelping and barking, as if that dog was begging us to come and see what he had caught or was about to catch.

So out we went, Little Jim's dad leading the way at first. Then, because I knew the swamp better than he did, he let me lead, and the rest followed me. I had a long flashlight in my hand. I knew just where to walk and not get off the trail into the slime and ooze.

Just then the flashlight showed me where Jeep was—behind a wild rosebush, and he was barking more excitedly than ever. In a few steps we were all there.

Then I let out a scream, which I certainly didn't intend to do but couldn't help because I saw something!

Something, I tell you. "Look!" I cried, and every nerve was trembling so much I dropped the flashlight. Then, of course, nobody could see till I'd picked it up again. I was so scared by now that I couldn't even yell. I held the flashlight out toward the place again, past the barking, panting dog, and saw it again.

"Look, everybody. Look! There's a—there's a man's head lying out there all by itself!"

8

I had never seen anything like *that* before in all my life—a man's head lying out in the middle of the swamp. My flashlight was focused straight on it, and I could see the eyes blinking and the lips moving. And then I heard a voice call, loud and frightened, "Help! *Help!*"

Well, what would *you* do if you saw somebody's head lying out in a swamp and you heard a voice calling, "*H-e-e-e-lp,*" and the voice sounded worse than Old Bawler's long, sad high voice trembling across the woods?

"*Help . . . help!*"

The dog was barking. Poetry was yelling. Little Jim's dad was talking. When Dragonfly saw the head, he was more excited than ever. He cried, "It's John Till! He's got off the path that leads through the swamp and has stepped off into the quagmire, and he's going down. We've got to save him!"

It looked like we had to do something and we ought to do it mighty quick! I looked at that little barking Airedale, who looked up and back at us with a worried expression on his face. At the same time he seemed to be saying, "I told you I wasn't any picayune! I told you I wasn't an insignificant person or thing!"

Well, not only did we see John Till's head

lying out there in the swamp—that's what it had looked like at first—but I knew he had done what Dragonfly said. He had stepped aside from the path, and now there he was, floundering around in the quicksand. The quicksand had slipped from under his feet, and he had gone down, down, down until he was in all the way to his neck. Then I saw his hands, and he was holding them out the way my baby sister, Charlotte Ann, holds out her hands to my mom when she is in her crib and wants to get out and can't and feels terribly unhappy. She reaches up to Mom to put down her nice kind arms and pull her out and up.

We knew it wasn't safe for us to get any nearer than Jeep was, so the only thing we could do for a minute was to stand there and argue with ourselves, deciding what to do.

Little Jim's dad said, "We ought to have a rope. We ought to have a tree or sapling, something to push out to him so he can catch hold of it."

None of us had an ax or hatchet with us, and we knew we wouldn't have time to take our knives and cut down a small tree and trim all the small branches off and push it out to John Till so he could grab it. All this time he was hollering for help because he was not only in all the way to his neck, but he was down so far that he had to keep his chin lifted or he couldn't even breathe.

We knew that most any minute he would slip under and that would be the end. He was struggling like a boy who is trying to swim and keep his head above the water and can't because he has cramps.

My brain generally works quicker when I am angry about something, but it started to work quick right that minute too, when I realized that something had to be done to save the man's life. I was thinking, what if he'd actually go down and his mouth would get filled with that awful quicksand and he would choke to death and he would have to leave his body and go somewhere to meet God. He would be lost forever on account of being stubborn and rebellious and not willing to bow his stubborn old will and confess that he was an honest-to-goodness sinner needing a Savior—the only One there is. And you know what *His* name is.

I felt sorry for Little Tom Till and for his big brother, Bob. They would miss their dad even if he had been mean to them. I felt sorry especially for the boys' mother, sad-faced Mrs. Till, who had a hard enough time to make a living as it was, although maybe it would be easier for her if John Till was dead and then—well, if he was dead, he wouldn't spend all the money he earned on himself. I remembered that sometimes my mom let Mrs. Till do our washing and paid her more than it was worth, so as to be kind to her.

Old John Till spent most of his money and his time in the combination pool hall and beer parlor in our town, and you never saw *him* in church. Not once!

"Here," Poetry said, "here's something that we could get out to him if we can do it." He slipped his hand into his pocket and out again with his knife. He opened the blade, while I held the flashlight for him, and in seconds he had a grapevine cut in two at its root.

You see, all around Sugar Creek, and especially around the swamp and down along the old bayou where we played, grapevines came out of the ground not far from the trees. Sometimes they actually grew holding onto the trees and then on up into the branches. In some places the grapevines were so long that they reached into the treetops. Well, I knew that Poetry had a good idea. The only thing was that we had to have a vine that was fifteen or twenty feet long or longer in order to save the man out there.

Of course, if we had wanted to, we might have made a rope out of *ourselves*. Poetry could have lain down on the ground, and I could have lain down at the end of his big feet and taken hold of them, and Dragonfly could have crawled out over us and held onto *my* feet, and . . . But that wouldn't have made a very strong rope, and we might have lost a boy as well as John Till.

I hesitated just a second, wishing Circus was there to go shinning up that red oak. He could have done it quick as a monkey and could have cut off the vine up there, and then we could have thrown it out to John Till in time to save his life. I thought all these things in less than half a minute. Then I did some quick acting, much quicker than I do when my dad tells me to do something I don't especially want to do and should.

I didn't have time to *think* anymore, because I was already on my way up that rough-barked oak tree. I held on as tight as I could, wrapping my legs around the trunk to keep from falling. Then I shoved one hand into my pocket to get hold of my knife. I didn't have it!

All this time John Till was hollering for help. All this time the picayune was barking, first at me up the tree, then at John Till, and then at the excitement. And all the time I was wishing I would hurry, and I couldn't. It was like being in a dream in which you are trying to get away from a mad bull and can't run. I was just hanging there, holding on.

Then Poetry yelled up to me, "You can have *my* knife!" He threw it up to me.

It came sizzling through the air, but I couldn't see it, and it dropped back into the leaves beside the footpath. Then Little Jim's dad sprang into action. He had his own knife in his hand, and right away he was on his way up the tree to where I was. He was almost as good a climber as Circus. He handed the knife to me, and before you could say "Jack Robinson Crusoe," I had that vine cut in two.

Little Jim's dad slid down the oak tree and in almost no time at all had the end of the vine out to where John Till was. He was not a bit deeper down, as if maybe he had managed to stay up by struggling.

John Till hooked his long fingers around that end of the vine like a drowning man clinging to a straw! We started to pull, all of us that could get hold of the other end. I did too, as soon as I was down the tree.

It looked good to see John slowly coming up a little and moving toward the safe place where we were. I was glad.

Then suddenly somebody hollered, "Hey! Hey! Where's Little Jim! He's *g-gone!*"

Poetry's yell unnerved us all so that for a second we forgot what we were doing. John Till started sliding back into the quicksand again. Little Jim gone? My head swam round and round and round. What on earth had happened? Had he slipped away while we weren't watching, or had he tried to go out there and get John Till and had slid into the quagmire himself?

I guess the excitement made us pull too hard on the grapevine then, for the very worst thing that could have happened *did* happen, and that was—well, I *heard* it before I could believe it. I *felt* it next, and then I *knew* it, because all of a sudden I lost my balance and stumbled backward over Dragonfly and Mr. Foote's foot, and we all landed in a heap on top of and underneath each other. *The grapevine rope had broken!*

9

It's a terrible feeling knowing you have to save a man's life or it will never be saved—knowing that if you don't do something, nothing will be done.

It's a worse feeling when all of a sudden, while you're saving the life of a man you don't like very well, you discover your best friend is gone, and you don't know where, and you think maybe you'll never see him again.

There we were with our broken vine, all in a jumble of legs and arms and bodies, with a dog barking so excitedly we couldn't think straight, and with everything upside down including ourselves, trying to think what to do next. There we were when from behind us I heard the sweetest music I'd ever heard in most of my life. It was Little Jim's voice, saying, "Here, Daddy! Here's one of the canvas curtains from the cave. We can make a rope out of that."

I felt so relieved that I jumped to my feet, whirled around, and made a dive for Little Jim and the canvas. I knew we'd have to cut it into strips and tie the strips together, twisting them so the new "rope" would be strong enough not to break.

But I whirled around so quick that I lost my balance and stepped too far to one side of our safe place, and the next thing I knew *I* was out in the ooze and water and mud. It felt as if I was also into the quicksand. I began to go down, down, down, feeling suction down there pulling on the bottoms of my feet. Right away I was in halfway to the top of my high boots, so I began to scream for help myself.

Poetry, who was standing closest to me, reached out his hand. I caught hold of it and managed to pull one of my feet out. It made a sucking noise, the way a cow's foot does when she pulls it out of about ten inches of mud in a very muddy barnyard. Almost right away I was back onto solid ground again, but I knew we didn't dare trifle with danger. It would be very easy for every single one of us to get out there, and every single one of us would go down.

It didn't take Little Jim's dad long to get a makeshift rope made out of that tough canvas.

We tossed one end out to where John Till could take hold of it.

"Hey!" I yelled to him. "Don't pull so *hard!*"

He was pulling and pulling as though he was scared half to death, and maybe he was.

Hand over hand, every one of us pulled. But Little Jim's dad and Poetry had the strongest grip on the canvas "rope." Steadily, steadily, we saw the man come up out of the mire. When we got him a little closer, he found solid ground under his feet. He was about waist deep at the time, right where I had been a little while before, so I knew now that I couldn't have gone all the way down.

I held the flashlight so that everybody could see. John Till was the strangest-looking person. He was absolutely covered with mud, a whitish, brownish, yellowish mud or clay or quicksand or whatever it was, from his chin to the toes of his boots. He still looked scared. And he must have been very cold, for he was trembling and trembling.

All of a sudden I remembered a Bible story I'd once read where a jail keeper was doing the same thing—trembling. He sprang through the jail door and said to Paul and Silas—the Christian men who had been staying in his jail because they had preached the gospel—he said to them, "What must I do to be saved?" That's a very important question, which anybody can answer by saying what Paul said to that scared jailer. What he said was, "Believe in the Lord Jesus, and you will be saved, you and your household," meaning a person's whole family can be saved the same way. And Paul wasn't talking about being saved from quicksand but about being saved forever and having eternal life.

I didn't get to think any more along that line. John Till was standing there shaking, so we knew we had to do something. Little Jim's dad said, "Well, John, your life has been saved. If you'll come along home with me, we'll get you some clean, dry clothes."

John Till stood still. There was the kind of sob in his voice that he'd had in the cabin. He said, "Mr. Foote, I made up my mind while I was down there—going down deeper and calling for help, and nobody heard me—I made up my mind that I was goin' to go straight. I made up my mind I wasn't goin' to live the kind of life I'd lived all these years. Made up my mind I was goin' to go to church. Made up my mind—"

He just stood there and shook and sobbed, and some more tears came out. One of them fell right down on his muddy right hand, the same hand that last summer had been all doubled up into a fist and had whammed me on the jaw and knocked the daylights out of me.

"Made up my mind," he went on with his voice choking, "that I was goin' to set an example for my boys. I was goin' to follow Jesus. I was goin' to be a good man and follow Jesus and go home to heaven."

I thought that was a wonderful thing. I guess I felt pretty good to hear a bad man say that.

So I was surprised to hear Little Jim's dad say, "That's wonderful, John. There are going to be a lot of people at Sugar Creek happy because of that. But do you know, John, that *that* won't save you?"

We all started then toward the Foote house because John Till was so cold. We took a short-cut through the woods, and all the way home Little Jim's dad explained things to him. You could hear our boots squishing and squashing. You could hear John Till's boots doing the same thing because they were full of water. It was pitiful to look at him with the mud all over him like that. I hoped the police wouldn't come and get him. I hoped he was really meaning business this time, that he was actually going to do what he said he was going to do.

One of the things Little Jim's dad said was, "Being good won't save you, John. You can't follow the example of Jesus and be saved that way."

All the rest of us were listening, not understanding it very well but knowing enough to keep still.

"It's this way, John," Little Jim's dad said. "Suppose, while you were down there in the quagmire all the way up to your chin, that I had stood on the safe solid ground and said to you, 'Look at me, John Till! Turn over a new leaf! Just follow me, and I'll take you home. See how tall and straight I am. See how I stand on this solid ground! Look at me and follow me along home!'"

John Till didn't say anything for maybe twenty-five feet of walking. All we could hear was the squishing and the crunching and the other noises our shoes and boots made as we hurried through the woods. We could hear the wet leaves scrunching under our feet. Now and then in a dry place we could hear the rattle of the dry ones, which reminded Poetry of a poem we had in our schoolbooks. We were far enough behind for him to quote it without disturbing Mr. Foote or John Till, so he said:

". . . the husky rusty, rustle
Of the tassels of the corn . . ."

Then we listened again to the men.

Mr. Foote was saying, "If I'd told you *that,* you'd have thought I was crazy. You see, you had to be saved first, and *then* you could follow me home."

Hearing that was just like turning on a small light in my mind. It was suddenly clear as broad daylight on a summer day exactly how to be saved. If anybody wanted to be saved and go to heaven and follow Jesus home, he never could do it until *after* he had been rescued. First, he had to be lifted out of a quagmire. I was explaining it to Little Jim the best I could, and I said to him, "You have to be lifted out of the quagmire of—" I kind of hated to say the word *sin,* even though it was a Bible word and everybody was a sinner.

Little Jim said to me across the top of a small rosebush, "First, you have to be saved from sin, and *then* you can follow Jesus." And I knew that little fellow had spoken the truth. Well, we could see the light in Little Jim's house, and then we could see Little Jim's mom sitting beside their radio. We knew that pretty soon we would be there.

At least I *thought* I saw Little Jim's mom sitting by the radio. I couldn't really tell, except that I knew their radio was near the window.

About that minute we came to a rail fence. All of us climbed over and down into a deep ditch, scrambled up through the long, tangled dead weeds, which in the summertime had been very green along the fencerow there, and reached the narrow road that goes up to Little Jim's house and then on past to the red-brick schoolhouse where all the Sugar Creek Gang goes to school.

There was a small hill that we had to climb before we came to the front gate. Then Mr. Foote opened the gate, and we were about ready to go in when the lights of a car came swinging up the road where we had just been.

The car was going very fast. It went *bangety-bang* across the wooden bridge that spans the small tributary that flows into Sugar Creek. When the car reached the lane that leads into the Footes' barnyard, it turned in and stopped all of a sudden, and a powerful, searchlight swung around in our direction and lighted up every one of us.

You could see us as plain as day, standing there by the narrow wooden gate just getting ready to go through.

"It's the police!" Poetry whispered hoarsely to me.

I expected John Till to get scared again and turn around and run. I thought he'd run down the road and dive under the bridge.

But John Till said, "It's—it's the police, and they're after me. It's all right. I'm ready to go. I'm ready to go!"

It was just as if he had heard the policemen in the car over there telling him to put his hands up, because he didn't wait. He shot both mud-covered hands right up in the air, swung back through the small gate, and started walking toward the light. He raised his voice and called to them, "I'm surrendering!"

A policeman stepped out of the car, walked over to him, snapped on a pair of handcuffs, and was going to make him get into the car.

Little Jim's dad spoke up then and said, "Men, John Till is ready to surrender to you, and he is willing to go to jail tonight, but he's been out in the swamp, and he's all covered with mud. I'd like to take him into our house and let him have a good warm bath, a lunch, and a change of clothes. I have a suit that he could wear, and then I'll bring him down to the jail to you as soon as he is ready, or I'll bring him down tomorrow morning. He can stay at our house all night if he wants to."

I knew that *Bob* Till was already living there, because he was paroled to Mr. Foote, and I started to wonder something but didn't get to finish it.

Well, most policemen are kind when they have to arrest people, even though they have to be very firm sometimes. Anyway, this one said, "He won't need to take any bath first. We have a shower down at the jail. And as for clothes, we have a striped suit down there which he can wear. John Till," he said, directing his words to very cold and quiet and trembling John Till, "climb into the back of the car there!" His voice was kind, but it meant business.

Mr. Till hesitated a moment. He looked over at Little Jim's dad. Then he looked around the circle at the rest of us, and in a very trembly voice—maybe trembling because he was still so cold or because he was still not over being frightened—he said, "Boys, I've never had any use for the Sugar Creek Gang up to this time, but you've proved to me that you are gentlemen. I'm proud to have my son Tom be a member of your gang. I'm proud of the way you've treated my boy Bob. And now I'm proud of the way you have treated me. I'm not goin' to forget it in a long time. I want to thank you. And now—"

John Till was still talking, but then he stopped. I could hear the rattle of the handcuffs on his wrists. I don't think I'd ever felt so sorry for a man in my life. I hated to see him receive the punishment he deserved, and yet there wasn't anything any of us could do about it.

I guess the weather had been clearing up all the time. But I was surprised when the moon came bursting out from under a bank of clouds and shone down through the leafless trees in the yard and on John Till's face. For some reason, I decided I liked John Till and was going to be kind to him. So I started to say something, but the words got stuck in my throat. I croaked like a frog when he is trying to holler in the spring along the creek and his voice chokes off and he sounds like a tin can that has been hit by a rock that some boy has thrown at it.

I did manage to say, though, "John Till— Mr. Till, Little Tom is one of my best friends. I like him very m-much."

Then the gruff-voiced policeman said, "All right, John Till! We'll can the sob stuff. Into the backseat there!"

John turned. There wasn't anything we could do, not a thing. We just had to stand there and watch him get in, listen to the door slam, hear the motor speed up as the driver stepped on the accelerator, and watch the big black car back out of the drive. Then we watched as it went forward and down the hill, across the little tributary bridge, and on up the hill on the other side of the valley. Pretty soon its two taillights looked like two tiny red stars at the top of the hill.

John Till was on his way to jail.

I didn't know till later that the reason John Till hadn't gone down all the way into the quicksand was that, when he got in up to his neck, his foot had struck a rock down there, and he'd been balancing himself on it. If his foot had slipped off while we were taking such a long time rescuing him, he'd have gone down for sure.

10

Yes, John Till was on his way to jail. And in a few minutes the Sugar Creek Gang—all there were with us at the time—were on our way home in Little Jim's dad's car. Not only that, but this Sugar Creek Gang story is on its way to the end. It won't be long now until I shall come to the very last word.

All the time I rode along in Little Jim's dad's sort of oldish car, I kept thinking about what my dad was going to say to Seneth Paddler when he called to see him the next day in his rustic old cabin in the hills.

I could see in my mind's eye that little log cabin with its clapboard roof and its back door down in the cellar. I could see the old flintlock on the wall. I could see the little cow's horn with a cap on the large end, which had been used for gunpowder a long time ago. I could see the clean-looking bed. I could see the stairway. I kept thinking about it all as we all rode along.

Little Jim was riding along with us. His dad had said he could if he wanted to. Dragonfly and Poetry sat in the backseat because they lived in the same direction as I did. We went across the noisy bridge that spanned the tributary and then followed the same trail that the police car had taken when its two red taillights had looked like two crimson stars at the top of the hill. On up, farther and farther up that little lane-like road we drove until we came to the cornfields across from our house.

We turned left at a tall, branching elm tree, which in the summertime had enough shade for many boys to play under. But we hardly ever played there. It wasn't a very friendly tree. Its branches were so very high, and its trunk was too large around for any of us boys to climb. Not even Circus had ever climbed it and didn't even want to. Every other tree along Sugar Creek seemed to belong to us and maybe had grown just for us, but this one *didn't* seem to belong.

We turned there, drove along the end of Dad's last year's cornfield, turned left in a little while, and went down the road to the Collins house. As I sat there in the front seat with Little Jim between me and his dad, looking down the graveled driveway to our house, I could see a light in the kitchen window. I knew that my mom and my dad would be awake waiting for me. I could hardly wait to tell them everything that had happened.

There is something good about coming home, something great.

Pretty soon, Mr. Foote's car was stopping beside our front gate, not far from the mailbox that had printed on it the words THEODORE COLLINS, which is my dad's name. The car lights shone on those letters, and I felt proud of my great big dad.

I climbed out of the car and said, "Good night, Mr. Foote. Thank you very, very much." Little Jim was so sleepy he was all slumped over beside his dad. Poetry and Dragonfly in the backseat were still awake, although I could tell by looking close into Dragonfly's dragonfly-like eyes that he was getting very drowsy.

For a minute I forgot all about having to have my teeth filled in the morning. I said, "So long, everybody." Then I turned and lifted the little latch that let me through our front gate. Dad had shut it as he always does at night.

I walked across the only footpath my folks will let me have across our yard, on account of Mom's wanting a nice grassy lawn, and came to the boardwalk that leads from our back porch steps to the pitcher pump maybe twenty feet away.

I lifted the pump handle, listened to it squeak as I shoved it down, and watched a nice stream of water come spouting out, sparkling in the moonlight. I watched the pretty little ripples it made in the tub out of which our horses drink sometimes. Sometimes old Mixy drinks from that tub.

I started toward the back porch steps. Then I stopped again and looked back toward the moon, which was sailing in a very pretty sky, and I thought about all the things I had been thinking about. Somehow or other as I looked at that big, beautiful, half-round moon with what looked like continents of different shapes on it, I thought about its being the same moon that would be shining on Old Man Paddler's cabin, the same moon that would be shining on the jail where John Till was right that minute taking a shower.

And then, looking at those dark places on the moon that looked like continents on a globe, I got to thinking that it was the same moon that would be shining down upon that little caterpillar-shaped island away down in the northern part of the Caribbean Sea. I got to thinking how nice it would be if I could go flying in an airplane above the clouds and under a moon like that with the ocean down below and with the whole Sugar Creek Gang sitting in the seats all around me. It felt good to imagine having a ride like that.

Pretty soon I heard the latch of our back door squeak. Then I heard the door open with the same noise it always makes. And then the screen door opened, and there was the same friendly squeaking in its springs. My dad's big voice, which nearly always sounds like a bull-frog's voice does along Sugar Creek, called to me and said, "Well, Bill Collins! Come on into the house." He said it so cheerfully.

I looked up, and there he was with his striped pajamas on. I was glad to see him.

Just as I came through the door and shut it, my mom called from the bedroom away on the other side of the living room. "Well," she said, "my boy is home again. Did you have a nice time? *No!*" She raised her voice a little to say that and then added, "Don't tell us now. I'm too sleepy. Wait till morning to tell us."

The way she said that made me want to start in and tell her everything that happened on our hunting trip. So I did start but was almost immediately interrupted by my dad. "Bill Collins, it's after midnight! You'll have to hurry or you won't get any sleep before the dentist starts grinding on your teeth at ten o'clock tomorrow morning!"

Wham! That was the way it felt to have him remind me of tomorrow morning.

"What?" I said. "What time did you say?"

My dad's deep voice laughed, and he said, "After you left, I called Dr. Mellen and told him that eight o'clock would be a bit early for you on Saturday if you were up late Friday night. So he looked over his appointments and telephoned back a little later. He said he'd had a cancellation. He said John Till was to come in at ten, but he didn't think he would be there, so—"

That started me to talking again, because I felt good to think I didn't have to get up so early, and even Mom felt better about it. Before I was through, I had talked and talked and talked. I had to wait till morning for some of it, though, because they didn't want me to wake up Charlotte Ann by mimicking the hounds and Jeep, which I had been doing every now and then in my story.

The morning was a wonderful morning. I

finished telling all the things I hadn't thought of the night before. By the time I was through, I had told my parents everything that you have already read.

Then Dad took me to the dentist's office.

"How long will it take?" he asked Dr. Mellen, who right that minute had me in the big chair with my mouth open and a small mirror with a handle on it moving around beside my teeth just before he started grinding.

Dr. Mellen looked at his watch and said. "Not long. Maybe thirty minutes."

"I'll wait," Dad said. And then he said to me. "You can go with me to see Old Man Paddler if you want to."

Well, I wanted to. *If the Sugar Creek Gang does get to go to a foreign country because Old Man Paddler sends us there,* I thought, *it'll be the first time in my life I've ever been out of the United States. It'll also be the first time I've been in an airplane above the ocean.*

Yes, I surely wanted to.

The *Sugar Creek Gang* Series: